BETWEEN TWO WORLDS

Other Apple Paperbacks you will enjoy:

BETWEEN TWO WORLDS

Candice F. Ransom

St. Mary of the Assumption School
3402 South Locust Road
South Bend, Indiana 46614

AN
APPLE
PAPERBACK

SCHOLASTIC INC.
New York Toronto London Auckland Sydney

ISBN 0-590-45755-1

12 11 10 9 8 7 6 5 4 3 2   4 5 6 7 8 9/9

Printed in the U.S.A.   40

First Scholastic printing, April 1994

Sarah Winnemucca, who lived from 1844 to 1891, was one of the first Native American women to speak out for Indian rights.

Winnemucca lived during the tumultuous period in which the white man invaded the domain of the Native American. At first the white man came to trap, trade, and prospect. Gradually, the whites took the land for farming, ranching, towns, and railroads.

Native American tribes of the Far West lived in the arid, mountainous region — in small groups with great spaces between camps. They migrated with the seasons, following pine-nut harvests and trout runs. When the white men herded the Native Americans onto reservations with no regard for their way of life, Sarah Winnemucca spoke up.

She was a Paiute, a tribe that permitted its women some freedom. Women could voice their opinions at council meetings, but they had to sit behind the men. The life of a Paiute woman was mainly confined to the cook-fire and the wickiup.

When she was young, Sarah traveled and went to school, both unheard of for a Paiute girl. She lived with white families and learned English. Moving back and forth between the two very different worlds cost Sarah her identity. She was not white, yet she was not a typical Paiute woman, either.

Sarah Winnemucca was much more than an Indian woman who could speak English. She was a gifted teacher. She was a passionate peacemaker. She was a hero.

Above all, Sarah was a spokesperson. She gave her people a voice.

A Note About Names

Sarah Winnemucca was born Thoc-me-tony, daughter of Winnemucca II. She later received the Christian name of "Sarah," possibly when she was twelve and staying with a white family. In her book, *Life Among the Piutes: Their Wrongs and Claims*, Sarah refers to herself and members of her family by their Christian names. To avoid confusion of multiple names, I have used the Christian names throughout this book.

Sarah belonged to a western tribe of Native Americans named "Paiute" (or "Piute") by the white men who first encountered them. Sarah's tribe referred to themselves as *Numa*, or simply, the People. Throughout this book I use the name of Numa, or the People, since this is Sarah's story.

Finally, in keeping with the terminology of the period, Native Americans are referred to as "Indians."

C.F.R.

A Note to the Reader

Sarah Winnemucca was a real person. Although her deeds have been documented in history, not much is known about her personal life.

Sarah wrote a book about her experiences called *Life Among the Piutes: Their Wrongs and Claims*. But there are gaps in this record: years are missing, some events are recounted briefly.

I have attempted to tell Sarah's fascinating story, as a story. This is a work of fiction. It is not a biography. The words are mine, but the action's are Sarah's.

— Candice F. Ransom

Part I

Sarah Winnemucca

1

Sarah stood at the edge of the marsh, one small fist scouring her eye, crying. Her older sister Mary was going off with her friends to gather bulrushes.

"I want to come, too," Sarah sobbed.

Her sister looked back and shook her head. "No, little sister. You are too small. Go back to Mother. She will be worried if you are out here alone."

Mary and her friends waded gracefully through the waist-deep water until they reached the little island where the best bulrushes and cattails grew in thick stands.

Sarah knew she was too small to wade through the water, but Mary could have carried her. Her older brother Natchez often carried Sarah, swooping her around and around so that she did not know sky from ground.

She turned away. Mary did not want to play with her. She had no time for a little sister.

Trudging back to camp, Sarah scuffed her feet

3

in the dust in front of their *karnee*. Her mother was sitting cross-legged in the doorway of the tule- and rush-covered lodge, grinding seeds. Her baby sister Elma dozed in her cradleboard as it swung gently from a low branch of a nearby mesquite tree.

"What is the matter, Sarah?" her mother asked, mashing the seed-paste in her *metate*, the shallow flat stone.

Sarah sat down with an undignified plop. "Mary won't let me play with her. She always leaves me. One day I'll be a big girl and I won't let Mary play with *me*."

"I know what you can do," her mother suggested. "Why don't you make your little sister a clay toy? Show me what a good animal you can make." She poured water from a basket jug into the red dust at Sarah's feet and mixed it until the dirt formed a clay ball.

Sarah dug her toes into the warm ashes of yesterday's fire and began molding the clay. "Will you tell me a story, Mother?"

"Would you like to hear one of your grandfather's stories?"

Sarah's grandfather had been gone a long time. He left when she wasn't much older than Elma and now she was four summers. Sarah couldn't even remember her grandfather, but she knew he was a great man, the chief of all the Numa. Right

4

now he was far away, somewhere over the western mountains, fighting in a war.

Using her special story-telling voice, her mother began, "In the beginning of the world, there was one family. This family had four children, two girls and two boys. One boy and girl were dark and the other boy and girl were light. For a while they all got along and were happy together, but then the children started quarreling. Their parents were not happy."

Sarah pulled the clay into the long ears of a jackrabbit. Was her mother unhappy because Sarah quarreled with Mary? All stories had a message, Sarah knew. It was how children learned the ways of the People.

Her mother went on. "The parents called the children together and said 'Why are you so cruel to each other? Do you not have everything your hearts' desire?' Then their father told them to leave his house forever. 'Go across the ocean and do not seek each other's lives.' "

Sarah shivered deliciously. Her mother recited the father's command in such a dramatic tone. "What did the children do then, Mother?" she asked.

"They disappeared and their parents saw them no more. After a while the dark children grew into a large nation. It is the one we belong to. And the light children grew likewise into a large nation. But one day — " Her mother's voice dropped. "One day, the light children will come meet us and then the healing of the old trouble will begin."

With a pointed stick, Sarah carved eyes and a smiling mouth. Her rabbit was finished. She set it on a rock so the sun would bake it hard and dry. Then Elma could play with it.

"Was that story Coyote?" she asked. Fables, or make-believe tales, were called "Coyote" stories.

"Your grandfather says it is true," her mother replied. "Did you like that story?"

"Yes, Mother." But Sarah wasn't sure she did. She much preferred stories about Coyote and Rabbit.

This story, about the two dark children and the two light children, disturbed her. If the dark children were getting along fine by themselves, why did the light children have to come back? Would the light children be like Mary and not want to play with the dark children?

Now her mother told Sarah that once, long before Sarah was born, her grandfather heard of a party of strange humans traveling over the mountains. He eagerly asked what the men looked like. Upon learning the strangers had pale faces and hairy faces, her grandfather cried, "My white brothers! My long-looked-for white brothers have come at last!"

Sarah said now, "I hope I never see a white person!"

"You probably will," her mother said. "Many white people come over the mountains now. More every day. Your father has seen a white person."

"He said they are ugly with hair on their faces and white eyes and white skin! He calls them owl-faces. I never, never, *never* want to see an owl-faced man," Sarah stated vehemently. She didn't even want to *hear* about white men, much less see one.

Yet, when rumors about the newcomers whirled around the evening fire, Sarah was crouched behind the shelter of her mother's back, drinking in every word.

She learned that another tribe was saying the white brothers killed everyone in their path. Just this past winter a band of white people trapped by blizzards in the mountain pass ate each other when there was no food to be found. This last story kept Sarah awake at night. The owl-faced men must be terrible monsters to kill and eat the flesh of their own people. If she ever saw one, why, she would die right on the spot!

She began to see owl-faced men in every wind-stirred dust cloud on the horizon. She saw them in the silent shadows of slant-winged hawks circling lazily overhead. Every menacing rock hid an owl-faced man. Every twisted mesquite tree could suddenly spring to life as an owl-faced man.

Why *did* they have to come back? Did it matter so much if the old trouble between the dark children and the light children was never healed? Why couldn't the world be as it was?

Sarah had no answers to her questions. But she knew, because she kept her ears open, that more and more white men were pouring over the eastern mountains, streaming across the People's land, on their determined path to the sea.

One day Sarah's father, Winnemucca, declared it was time to gather food for the coming winter. "We will hunt and fish and gather seeds," her father decreed during his morning speech.

He was head chief in Sarah's grandfather's absence. Winnemucca stood in the doorway of his lodge and spoke loudly so that everyone could hear as they went about their morning tasks.

"We will store food and then we will go into the mountains for the winter. The white men are coming. They will not stop coming. We will not hope that the stories about these people are false. We will go into the hills to save our lives."

Sarah's father waited for the response to this announcement. At last everyone answered, "Yes." The chief nodded. They would start that very day.

Sarah went with her mother to gather seeds.

She beat the tall grasses with a paddle-shaped basket used for this purpose. Whacking the grasses vigorously with the seed-beater, she knocked the seeds into a small basket. A lot of the seeds fell on the ground instead of into her basket, but Sarah enjoyed feeling useful.

Ahead of her, Mary worked alongside her friends. Elma's cradleboard was slung across her mother's back. Sarah could see the small dark head bobbing as her mother beat the grasses with her paddle. At least Sarah wasn't the youngest on this expedition.

While the women gathered seeds, the men fished in the lake or stalked rabbit and other small game. Women dried the fish and ground the seeds on their stone *metates*, with grinding stones called *manos*. The food was stored in a large mound in a special location they could get to easily when the winter snows came. The mound was covered with grass and then mud, protected from weather and marauding animals. Now they could move to the mountains.

One morning, as Sarah was helping her mother pack their belongings in baskets, a cry rang out through the camp.

"White men are coming!"

White men! Coming here! Terror arrowed through Sarah's heart. Her mother's face was pinched with fright. She snatched up Elma and grabbed Sarah's hand.

People ran like spooked antelopes, heading for the nearby hills with only one purpose: to hide from the white men.

Sarah's mother dragged her along. The baby clung to her neck and her little feet joggled as Sarah's mother ran.

"We must hurry!" she ordered Sarah. "Pick up your feet!"

But Sarah could not move. She was rooted to the earth with fear. All she could think about was the white men who would kill them and then sit down and have a feast.

"Move, child!" her mother shrieked, nearly pulling Sarah's arm out of the shoulder socket.

Just then Sarah's aunt came panting up, towing Sarah's cousin in a similar manner.

"My daughter won't run!" her mother cried.

"Neither will my girl," said her aunt.

"What will we do?" Sarah's mother sounded desperate. "We must hide from the white men!"

"I know," said Sarah's aunt. "Let us bury our girls. They will be safe and we can run with the others. We must be quick or we shall be killed and eaten up!"

Sarah's mother and aunt swiftly scraped two shallow holes in the loose sandy soil. They instructed Sarah and her cousin to lie in the holes. Sarah lay flat on her back, too frightened to understand what was happening. Then her mother

10

began clawing earth over her. Sarah cried out, panicked. She was being buried alive!

"Hush, little one!" her mother said. "I will not cover your face with dirt, only your body, so you will be hidden from the white men."

Her mother placed sagebrush over Sarah's face so she would be shielded from the fierce sun and the white men. Sarah's aunt did the same to her daughter.

"We will come back for you when it is safe," Sarah's mother promised. "Be quiet and the white men will not know you are there."

Then the two women fled, leaving the girls buried. And alone.

Sarah's heart pounded under the weight of sand covering her chest. Though her face was thrust into the scratchy branches of the sagebrush, her arms, legs, and body were buried. She could not move, even if she wanted. She was so frightened, she could barely breathe.

Next to her, her cousin sobbed quietly. She was afraid, too. How long would they have to lie in their graves? What if the white men came and found them anyway?

The day passed in an agony of silence. Sarah was very thirsty. She imagined it was raining, and opened her mouth to receive the blessed drops. But it wasn't raining. She had dozed and had been dreaming. Her throat was parched.

Once a chuckwalla lumbered across her chest. She felt the swish of its tail and bit back a scream. At first she thought it was a white man, digging her up to eat her.

"My legs hurt," her cousin whispered once.

"Mine, too." The muscles in Sarah's legs twitched the way a snake jumped after its head had been cut off.

"I wish I had run now," she confessed to her cousin.

"Me, too." Her cousin's voice sounded weak.

The sun coursed on its overhead journey, then sank out of sight. Night stole over the land, like the shadow of an eagle.

Sarah began to cry. She could not help it. She was so thirsty and hungry and her legs hurt so much.

"Oh, Father," she whimpered. "Have you forgotten your daughter? Are you never coming for me?" Tears mixed with sweat and grime, adding to her misery.

She fell asleep, certain she would die in her own grave. Some time later, she was awakened by whispering. The white men! Her heart thumping, Sarah heard footsteps drawing nearer. She held her breath . . . and then someone said, "They are right here."

She knew that voice! It was her mother!

Hands scrabbled at the dirt. Her mother yanked the sagebrush away from her face. When she was free, Sarah sat up, sobbing. She had never been so happy to see her parents in her entire life! Her cousin was being dug up by her aunt and uncle.

Sarah's father massaged the cramps from her legs until she could walk. "You have been very brave, daughter," he praised.

"Next time," Sarah said. "I will run when Mother tells me to!"

"I believe you have learned a lesson," said her father. To her mother, he added, "Our daughter is quick of speech for one so young."

Sarah wondered if being quick of speech meant that she was special. Her mother and father were careful not to favor any of their children over the others.

Yet she sensed that in some way she was different.

2

Sarah carefully selected a sumac shoot from the pile at her feet and snapped off the upper part. Placing the shoot between her teeth, she bit down hard. Instead of splitting into three pieces, the branch was a mass of mangled twigs.

Sighing, she selected another shoot and tried again. Basket making was not as easy as it appeared. Mary could split willow and sumac shoots slicker than a rabbit's whisker. Her sister's baskets were marvels of beauty, with the soul of the wood shining through. Mary's skill at basket weaving had brought her fame and their mother had remarked more than once that Mary would be much sought-after when she became of marriageable age.

Sarah had only been making baskets since summer. The seed basket she had fashioned for her mother was so full of holes, the seeds dribbled out. Yet her family never made fun of Sarah's attempts. It was not the way of the People to make cruel jokes.

Now her mother glanced over at Sarah's pile of unusable sumac splits and nodded encouragingly.

"Keep trying, child. Remember, no one ever does anything perfectly the first time."

Sarah bit a few more shoots, secretly wishing there was *some*thing she could do perfectly. At five summers, she ought to be able to do simple jobs well. But Sarah's attention wandered, resulting in minor calamaties.

Just yesterday, her mother gave her some seeds to grind. While tipping the basket onto the *metate*, Sarah was distracted by a buzzard soaring overhead. She wondered how the great bird could fly so long without flapping his wings, never noticing she had poured the seeds onto the ground.

Her mother had noticed and scolded her gently. "Keep your mind on your work, Sarah. You can watch the bird later."

But she wanted to watch the bird *then*. Grinding seeds was not so important. The women ground seeds nearly every day of their lives. In fact, it seemed that all the women ever did was prepare food and take care of babies. The men went hunting and fishing and saw the world. The women stayed close to the lodges, tending fires, cooking meals, and minding children.

Sarah envied her brother, Natchez, who had

recently become a man. Like the other boys, Natchez had been hunting small game since he was old enough to shoot an arrow. But in accordance with the ways of the People, he was not permitted to eat the game he killed. This summer Natchez was able to handle a larger bow. He strode boldly off one day, armed with his new bow and eagle-feathered arrows, and returned with the hide of his first important kill, a mountain sheep.

It was a great day. Chief Winnemucca cut the hide into a long snakelike coil. Natchez stood proudly with his quiver on his back, while his father threw the looped hide over him. Then Natchez jumped through the loop five times, as the ritual dictated. Winnemucca clapped him heartily on the shoulder and the rest of the tribe came forward to offer congratulations.

Around the fire that night, Natchez grinned at Sarah, grease smearing his chin. She grinned back. For the first time, her big brother was permitted to eat the meat from his kill. He could do whatever he liked, for he was now a man.

Her brother joined the older men on hunting and fishing expeditions. Sometimes he went off by himself, on mysterious missions that filled Sarah with longing and envy. She knew Natchez was out seeing the world. Her own world stretched no farther than the camp and her mother's sight.

"You are growing weary," her mother said now, observing her daughter's flagging enthusiasm. "Put the basket-making things away for another day. We have all winter to weave baskets. Soon we will go to the mountains for the pine-nut harvest."

Sarah brightened at this news. She loved the oily nuts of the one-leafed pine tree. They tasted better than anything to her, even mountain sheep.

They left a few days later. Everyone in the tribe went to the pine-nut forests. The men hunted deer while the women gathered nuts. They used long branches to knock down the pinecones, which they collected in baskets. The cones had not yet opened, so at night Sarah and the other little girls flung pinecones into the fire. The heat caused the cones to open and release the nuts.

It was a good harvest year. Sarah and her family gave thanks to the Spirit Father who had led them to trees with an abundance of cones. Sarah's mother would grind the nuts into meal, which would then be boiled into mush or patted into cakes and baked over the coals.

Sarah was glad her mother was so clever with whatever food was at hand. It was a noble task. But deep inside, Sarah wished she could somehow escape a lifetime bent over a cook-fire. There was more to the world. She hoped she would be fortunate enough to see it.

One autumn day, when a long wind prowled

through the valley, Sarah's father joyfully announced that his father, Sarah's grandfather, was at last coming home.

Sarah thought this was going to be a great day, like the day that Natchez became a man. Her grandfather had been gone such a long time, more than three summers — longer than Sarah could remember.

Everyone in Sarah's tribe — old men, little babies strapped to cradleboards, small children clinging to their mothers' hands — walked down the sandy ridge to greet the chief of all the Numa. Signal fires spread the news far and wide. People from other parts of the country arrived on horseback and on foot. They all sang a welcoming song.

Sarah hung back when she saw a group of men on snorting horses. They had a look in their eyes that spoke of the wonders they had seen and another look that hinted at the horrors of war.

Her mother pointed out a tall man wearing a dark blue garment with brass buttons. "That's your grandfather."

The tall man rose in his stirrups to speak to his people. "I am Captain Truckee. That is the name given to me by my white brother General Fremont. Call me by that name from now on."

Sarah did not understand why her grandfather, who had a perfectly good name, wanted to be called Captain Truckee now. *Truckee* meant "very well" in the language of the People. She supposed her grandfather had performed very well in the service of this General Fremont and the general gave him a new name.

As Captain Truckee talked, Sarah learned that he had been to a country called California, a beautiful land over the far mountains, settled by white men. Her grandfather and several other men served as guides to the white soldier named Fremont and later helped him in the war with Mexico.

They went back to camp. Natchez rode on the back of Captain Truckee's horse. Sarah walked with her mother and her sisters. She was a little afraid of her grandfather. She wasn't sure why. Maybe it was the dark blue garment, the soldier's coat, he wore.

That night around the evening fire, her grandfather told the People of his adventures. He had observed many wonderful things and brought back two of them. From a secret fold in the dark blue coat, he took out a small white square, which he magically unfolded into a large white square. Everyone stared with curiosity.

"This is my paper-friend," he said. "It can talk to me and I can talk to it in return. My paper-friend can talk to all our white brothers, and our white sisters, and their children."

Sarah's father grunted as he gingerly held the white square. "It does not speak to me. I hear nothing."

Captain Truckee took back the precious white

square and folded it carefully into a small square again. "That is because you do not know how to listen to it. My friend can travel like the wind. It can go away from here to our white fathers and brothers and sisters and come back to tell what they are doing."

Puagant, the medicine man, gestured with his pipe. "What does your paper-friend say?"

"It says," replied Captain Truckee, "that I am a great friend of General Fremont and that our people are friends of our white brothers and we mean them no harm. All I have to do is show this paper and it will tell anyone this truth."

Sarah ached to touch her grandfather's paper-friend, to hear the white square speak to her. Would it tell her a new Coyote story?

"And what is the second wonderful thing you brought back to show us?" Winnemucca asked Captain Truckee.

As if on signal, Captain Truckee and several other men went to their packs and drew out long, thin, hide-covered bundles. The bundles contained shiny black sticks.

"The weapons that sound like thunder," Winnemucca said.

"Guns," Captain Truckee corrected him.

The men immediately clamored for a demonstration of the white man's guns.

"Take the children into the hills," Truckee commanded. "The guns make a fearful noise and might even kill one of them."

Sarah fled into the hills with her mother and the other women and children. The guns *did* make a fearful noise, worse than thunder. Sarah huddled on the ground, her hands clapped over her ears, and shrieked with each shot. All the children were screaming. At last her mother and the other women stormed back into camp, demanding the men stop shooting or their children would die of fright.

Sarah's mother came back for her. "Come now, Sarah. The men have promised to stop making that terrible racket."

Sarah shrank from her mother's grasp. "Oh, Mother! Please don't make me go back!" she cried.

Her mother took her arm. "Did I not tell you it was safe?"

But Sarah didn't believe her. She would *not* go back to camp, not as long as her grandfather brandished a thunder-stick. She did not want to die. With all her might, she fought her mother and even bit her.

Her mother left, bringing back her father. Sarah tried to kick and bite Winnemucca but he scooped her into his arms and carried her back to camp. Now Sarah was both afraid and ashamed. She buried her face in her father's chest.

A voice said, teasingly, "Is that young lady

ashamed because I have come to see her? Aren't you glad to see me?"

Sarah knew her grandfather was speaking to her and refused to look up.

"Well," her grandfather said in a resigned tone. "If she does not love me anymore, then I shall have to take my gun and kill myself."

Sarah burst into fresh tears. She sobbed harder than any baby, crushing her wet face into her father's neck. She cried so hard, her mother took her from her father's arms and walked back into the hills. They did not return until the next day. Sarah's shame ran deep. She was angry with her grandfather for teasing her and making her act like a baby. She would not look at him. When he spoke to her, she stared stonily at the ground.

At night, she sat apart from him when he told stories about white men. But she listened to every word, fascinated. He told them about the moving houses and the houses that traveled on the ocean. The water-houses were faster than horses and higher than the hills surrounding their camp.

"Surely such a house would sink," said Winnemucca skeptically.

"It is every word truth," Truckee insisted. "Our white brothers are a mighty nation. They have a gun that can shoot a ball bigger than your head, that can go farther than that mountain over there." He pointed to a peak twenty miles away.

He sang the soldier-songs, which everyone

thought were very funny. And he taught them the words to a song called "The Star-Spangled Banner." Sarah loved that song. All that winter, she sang "The Star-Spangled Banner." The words were so beautiful, even though she had no idea what they meant.

One day her grandfather pulled out his paper-friend. Sarah scooted closer for a better look.

Her grandfather pretended not to see her sidling up to him. "I wonder if that young lady would like to see my friend? If she speaks to me, I might show it to her."

Sarah shyly put her hand on her grandfather's arm. "I would like to see the paper-friend, Grandfather," she whispered.

He put the wondrous document into her hands. Sarah studied the markings, waiting for the friend to speak to her.

"You will have to learn to talk to it," her grandfather said. "You must learn to talk on paper like our white brothers. There will be more and more white men coming. This will be a good thing to know, this talking on paper."

Sarah held the paper importantly. Of all the people in the tribe, Captain Truckee wanted *her* to learn the paper-friend language. From that moment on, Sarah was no longer mad at him.

That spring, Winnemucca and Captain Truckee headed a fishing excursion on the Humboldt

River. Emigrants had been rolling steadily into the valley, now that the fierce winter was over. While the People were peacefully fishing, a party of white men fired on them.

Sarah stood at the doorway of her wickiup, her fist crammed in her mouth, as the fishing party limped into camp. Draped over the saddles of their horses were two of her uncles and several other men. Her father hefted his brother over his shoulder. Blood trickled from her uncle's mouth and his eyes stared unseeingly at the sky. He was dead, killed by a white man.

All that night Puagant prayed and chanted over the wounded. Sarah's uncle Wa-he recovered — five of the injured men did not.

Winnemucca called a council. He wanted to kill the white settlers living near the river for the murder of his brothers.

Sarah's grandfather wept. "Is not my dear beloved son laid alongside the dead? I know and you know that those men who live at the river are not the ones who killed our men. How dare you ask me to let your hearts be stained with the blood of those who are innocent of the deed that has been done to us by others."

Sarah watched, round-eyed, as the widow of her uncle cut off her hair. She braided her long hair and laid it across the breast of her dead husband. Then Sarah's mother and father cut off their long hair also. With arrows, they gashed their arms and legs. All the relatives of the dead men cut off their hair in mourning, and slashed their arms and legs, so their blood would mingle with the blood of the dead. Mourning hung over the camp like a black cloud.

The medicine man turned to Captain Truckee. "The white brothers can do wonderful things. They can talk on paper and commune with the heavenly spirits. Yet your white brothers make your people's hearts bleed. Their blood is all around us, and the dead are lying all around us, and we cannot escape it. We cannot drive them away."

Captain Truckee faced Puagant squarely. "Remember the story of the four children. The light children have come back to live with the dark children. We must learn to get along with the whites. The only way to do that," he concluded emphatically, "is to go live among them."

As Winnemucca and other men stared incredulously at him, Captain Truckee continued, "Yes, we must go to the land of California and learn the white man's ways."

Sarah listened to her grandfather's words with bottomless shock. They were going to stay with the owl-faced men!

3

L ate that autumn, when the wind brought
nightly hints of snow and cold weather to
come, the People prepared to go to California.
Thirty members of the tribe were making the
journey. Chief Winnemucca, Sarah's father, was
staying behind, along with his best hunters and
women and men too old to travel.

Sarah's mother begged Captain Truckee to let
her stay behind, too. She did not want to leave
her husband.

"You must come," Captain Truckee insisted.
"You can return in the spring to be with your
husband. I want you to see the beautiful land of
California."

Sarah heard her mother weeping softly. Even
though Sarah was very young, she knew her
mother cared for her father deeply.

Her mother put Sarah's basket hat on her head,
talking about her courtship with Sarah's father.

"Your father had been coming to my grandmother's wickiup and sitting at my feet for nearly a year before I made up my mind that he would be my husband."

"What did he say to you?" Sarah asked.

"Nothing. A young man interested in a young lady never speaks directly to her." Sarah remembered then that her sister Mary did not speak to any males in the tribe except her father, brothers, uncles, and boy cousins. "Your father was so strong and handsome that I decided to be his bride. I cannot leave him," her mother said.

"Then we will stay here," Sarah said simply. "I do not want to see any owl-faced men."

It did not matter what Sarah wanted. She was only a little girl. And her mother had to obey Captain Truckee. They left the camp at daybreak. Sarah wept as she rode behind her mother, clasping her mother's waist.

That night they camped at Carson Sink, and the next night along the Carson River. On the third day, as they followed the white men's trail along the river, two of Truckee's scouts came back to report there were white brothers' wood-houses just ahead. Frightened, Sarah clung to her mother. Owl-faced men! Perhaps her grandfather would be afraid, too, and they would run and hide.

But Captain Truckee ordered his party to halt while he went to see his white brothers. When he came back a short time later, he brought some hard white cakes. "White man's bread," he said, distributing the bread among his people.

Sarah refused to eat any. Her brother Natchez teased her. "It is very, very good." He chewed heartily, as if the bread were the best food he had ever tasted. "You do not know what you are missing."

At the next encampment, white men and women hurried out to offer presents: red shirts for the men, calico cloth for the women. Mary received a beautiful white girl's dress. Captain Truckee brought back beef and more bread for everyone.

Sarah did not get anything. She dove under her brother's robes and did not come out even when her mother missed her and called her. Only when her mother began to cry did Sarah crawl out.

Her grandfather scolded her. "Our white brothers love good children, but not bad ones."

Shamefaced, Sarah stared at the ground. She wished she had never come on this awful trip. If only she could have stayed home with her father. She did *not* want to see any owl-faced men, no matter what her grandfather said.

White men's wood-houses were all along the trail. Sarah was amazed at the lodges that rolled on wheels. But whenever they came near a white man's settlement, Sarah, who was now riding behind Natchez, hid her face in his robes and cried.

Captain Truckee stopped at every camp to show his paper-friend. On one of his trips back from visiting his white brothers, he held the paper high and kissed it. "Oh, we should be lost without this," he said. "Let us mount up. Tonight we will camp by our white brothers, or near them. I have a child who is dying of fear of my white brothers."

Sarah knew her grandfather meant her. She could not help it. Didn't he know the owl-faced men would kill and eat them? How could her grandfather risk all their lives?

They crossed the lonely open land of the Great Basin, still breathlessly hot at midday. Beyond the desert rose the strange forbidding shapes of lava flats. Their ponies skirted petrified puddles of black glass and threaded their way through jutting, narrow-walled canyons. There was little grass to graze their horses. Captain Truckee urged them to cross this barren country quickly.

They did not see any more white man's wood-houses until they reached the head of the Carson River. Again, white men and women came forth to greet them. Captain Truckee stopped his party and rode back to where Sarah was riding behind her mother.

"Give me the baby," her grandfather said to her mother.

Sarah, hiding under her mother's robes, peeped

out to see her grandfather take baby Elma. "Not my sister!" she shrieked. "Mother, do not let him take her away!"

"No harm will come to your sister," her grandfather reassured her. "Watch, you will see."

But Sarah could not watch. She dove back under the robes. Then she heard her baby sister's shy giggle. She lifted her head. The white women were giving something small and white to Elma and Natchez.

"What is that?" Sarah's mother asked Captain Truckee.

"*Pe-har-be*," he replied. "Sugar."

One of the women approached their horse and held out the small hard lump toward Sarah, still cowering under the robe.

"Take it, my child," her grandfather prompted.

Reaching out from the robe, Sarah took the sugar lump, but she kept her face buried in the folds of the robe. She was proud of herself. She had obeyed her grandfather's wish and still did not look upon an owl-faced person! As they rode away, she sucked on the hard white lump. It tasted delicious! At last she, too, had received a present from a white person. Her heart lifted a bit.

Her grandfather trotted beside her. He shook his head with despair. "You must not be afraid of our white brothers."

"I cannot help it," she said. "They look so ugly."

And I will not gaze upon one, she promised herself.

But the next day her vow was shattered.

They had camped near a white man's woodhouse. Captain Truckee went down with some of his men to visit, as usual. Soon they came back, carrying large boxes. To Sarah's horror, two white men were *with* them.

There were no robes to dive under, no place to hide. She danced around her mother, wild with panic. "Mother!" she cried frantically. "What shall I do! They are coming here!"

Her grandfather's voice rang out. "Make a place for our guests to sit."

Sarah ducked behind her mother's skirts. When she ventured to look, the white men were only a few feet away. She screamed at the sight of their hairy faces, their pale ghostly eyes.

Her mother was angry at Captain Truckee. "I wish you would send your brothers away. They are scaring my child to death."

"She has at last looked upon our white brothers," her grandfather chuckled. "She will live."

But Sarah did not think she would. She cried the whole time the men talked with her grandfather and cried harder when all the other children, even Elma, ran up to the men to receive lumps of sugar.

She cried until her grandfather picked her up and rocked her and her sobs subsided into hiccups.

"Grandfather," she asked. "Can we go home?"

"No, dear one. We have not yet reached California," he replied. "I want you to see that beautiful land. You, especially, of all my son's children. I want you to know the ways of the white people. You will be able to talk on paper. It is a gift I believe you have. Will you try to get along with the white people, my child?"

Sarah felt safe in her grandfather's arms. The threat of white people seemed very far away. He believed she possessed the gift to talk to his paper-friend, which meant she was special indeed.

"Yes," she murmured sleepily. "I will try to make friends with your white brothers." She fell asleep before she could ask him if his white brothers would try to make friends with her, as well.

4

Sarah did not hide under her mother's rabbit-skin robes when they rode into Sacramento. There was so much to see, she forgot her fears. The white man's town was filled with wondrous sights.

A wide dirt trail went through the town, straight as the part in her mother's hair. Smaller trails branched off the main trail at right angles. Sarah's grandfather told her the neat trails were called streets.

Dozens of different wickiups lined the streets. Her grandfather pointed out one lodge where goods were sold and another that housed smaller lodges within, called a hotel. There were several lodges where fire-water, the white man's spirited drink, was sold. The Numa did not touch fire-water. Often white men became mean after drinking whiskey and the Numa did not believe this was the way to behave.

In Stockton, Sarah saw many wood-houses rolling along the streets, pulled by horses or mules. She could have stayed in the center of the main street and looked about her all day.

"We cannot stay here," her grandfather said. "We will camp outside of the town. But do not fret, my child. We will be here for the winter."

They had traveled all day and were weary. When they had located a campsite overlooking the river, Captain Truckee ordered the men to unsaddle the ponies and hobble them so they would not run off in the night.

"We will go to sleep without making any fire," he instructed. "Listen for the water-house's whistle. You will hear it at daybreak."

In the darkness, Sarah stumbled in the brush as she tried to find a place for her sleeping robe. She was very tired but could not sleep. She kept waiting for daybreak, so she could hear the water-house's whistle. She did not want to miss that beautiful sound.

But she fell asleep anyway and woke only when her mother shook her. She jumped up, blinking sleep from her eyes. The high sun told her it was late morning.

Sarah was starving, since they had gone to bed without any supper the night before.

"Look what I have brought." Natchez held out a large piece of cake. "This is sugar-bread. It is very good."

Sugar-bread was the tastiest white people's

food by far. Sarah ate the piece Natchez gave her, then ate more when her mother wasn't watching. She munched the delicious treat while waiting for the next water-house to come down the river. Her arms and legs itched. She scratched them, then rubbed her eyes when the warm sun made her drowsy. She did not want to miss the water-house again. But she did not feel well. Her head drooped on her bent knees. Soon she felt very ill.

When her grandfather returned that evening, Sarah lay tightly cocooned in her rabbit-skin robe, wracked with chills.

Her mother stroked her forehead and wept. Sarah opened her eyes and saw her grandfather's blurry face hovering anxiously over her.

"What is the matter with her?" he asked Sarah's mother.

"It was the sugar-bread your white brother gave us," her mother accused. "It was poisoned! My poor little girl will die and it is the fault of your white brother!"

"Open your eyes, my dear, and see your grandfather," he urged.

With great effort, Sarah dragged her eyelids open. Her grandfather gazed intently into her eyes. Her head felt as big as a mountain, it ached so.

"Can there be anything done for her?" her mother asked.

"Dear daughter," Captain Truckee said to her.

"I have eaten some of the sugar-bread, and so have you, and so did all the rest of us, and we are not ill. Did you bless the food before you gave it to your child?"

Her mother sobbed louder. Among the Numa it was a law that all strange food be blessed before it is eaten.

Even half-drowned in fever, Sarah knew her mother had not blessed the sugar-bread. She heard the People gather around her to pray. Their soothing voices comforted her as they begged the Great Father to let her get well. The sound closed over her ears like deep water and she was carried down a black river where all was nothing.

Her father always told her that an angel watched over the sick to take the soul to the Spirit-Land. Sarah could not see, but she felt the soft touch of the angel and heard her voice chant strange words. In her delirium, Sarah repeated the words.

"Poor little girl, it is too bad." Sarah spoke the strange language with no difficulty, even though she was gravely ill. She focused on the words and gradually began to feel better.

At last she was able to pry open her eyes a slit. The light hurt and she shut her eyes again, but not before she had glimpsed her mother silhouetted against the sky.

"Mother," she said. "What was the angel saying to me?"

"Oh, Father!" her mother cried. "My little girl is talking to the angels — she is dying!"

Sarah struggled to sit up. "I am not dying. I am better. I want to see the angel who talked to me so sweetly."

Her grandfather leaned over her, smiling. "That is my white sister. She has made you well. She put some medicine on your face and made you see again." He moved aside and a woman stepped forward.

Sarah thought the woman was truly beautiful, with fair hair and blue eyes. The woman put her hand on Sarah's forehead and spoke in the strange language.

"What is she saying, Grandfather?" Sarah asked.

"She is saying you have been a very sick little girl indeed. You were not poisoned by the sugar-bread, but by a plant called poison oak. You touched the plant and it made you ill."

Every day the woman visited Sarah. Once she gave her a dress. Sarah touched the bright calico. She couldn't wait to put it on.

But when the woman left, Sarah's mother snatched up the dress. "That dress belonged to her dead child. It must be burned."

Sarah began to cry. She knew the law of the

People, that all clothes and belongings of the deceased must be destroyed. But she so wanted to wear that dress!

When Sarah was better, they left Stockton and went to the ranch of one of her grandfather's white friends, Mr. Scott. Here they would stay the winter, Captain Truckee told them.

The men went up into the nearby hills to help with the cattle, leaving the women and children behind. They would cook and keep house for the ranch hands. Sarah's mother protested the arrangement, but Captain Truckee assured them they would all be safe.

Her mother led Sarah, Elma, and Mary into the house and they sat down on the floor. Her sisters cast their eyes downward with shyness, but Sarah gazed boldly around. What strange things she saw! Something high and long, and around it, red things.

She whispered to Mary, "Do you know what those are for?"

Mary replied importantly, "That high thing is what they use when eating, and the white cups are what they drink black hot water from, and the red things you see are what they sit upon when they are eating."

One of the red things was near Sarah. If only she could sit upon it she would be so happy! She asked her mother, "Can I sit on that one?"

Her mother shook her head. "No, they might

whip you. Remember what your grandfather said about touching things that do not belong to us."

Sarah was astonished to learn the white people whipped children. It was not the way of the People to physically punish their children for misdeeds. She did not want to be whipped, yet she thought she would die if she could not sit on the red chair.

Then Natchez entered with some other men. A white woman cleared the table and set more places. Natchez offered a chair to his mother. "And you, sister," he said to Sarah, "sit here."

The red chair! She was going to sit on it and not get a whipping! She sat gingerly upon the polished seat, twisting around to gaze at the picture painted on the back of the chair. It showed a scene of white birds and a yellow-rayed sun.

Food was set before her, and a cup of the black hot water. Sarah sipped the drink but did not like it.

Natchez told their mother what she and the girls would do all winter. They would wash dishes and cook. The white woman would teach Mary how to sew. Sarah knew her mother was afraid to be left alone, but they had to obey Captain Truckee's wishes.

The weeks passed. Sarah learned the names of the objects in the kitchen, like table and chairs. She picked up the white man's language and ways quite easily. She played with the other children and was happy in the white man's house.

But her sister Mary was not.

"Mother," Mary complained one night. "Those men say things to me. I know I am not permitted to speak to any male that is not my relative." Then she whispered something to her mother, who was cooking stew in the fireplace.

Their mother immediately sent for Captain Truckee. Natchez came since Captain Truckee was away in the mountains.

"Take this message to him," Sarah's mother said. "Tell him we must get away from here. The men he calls his brothers ride into camp and ask me to give my child to them. Tell him they come in at night and make us scream."

Sarah didn't know about this. She went to sleep every night, holding the baby, Elma. She thought everyone was as happy with the white people as she was.

Natchez left in a whirl of dust to find his grandfather. A few days later, Captain Truckee rode into camp. Sarah's mother ran to him, holding out her hands. "Father, let me take my children back to their father, where they will be safe."

"I will send for a wagon," Sarah's grandfather said sadly. He had so wanted his people to get along with his white brothers.

The wagon was packed. Sarah jumped around, excited to be going home in a wood-house.

"Are you glad we are going to ride in that beautiful red house?" she asked Mary.

"No," Mary said vehemently. "I hate everything that belongs to the white dogs. I would rather walk all the way, I hate them so!" Then she burst into tears.

Sarah stopped hopping around. She did not understand why her sister and mother were crying. She had had a good time, playing with the other children, learning words in the white man's language.

As they climbed into the wagon, Sarah looked back at the house. Silently she said good-bye.

5

As their party crossed the mountains into their homeland, they were met by one of the men who had stayed behind. He had grave news: Many of the People were dead. One by one, men, women, and children had fallen sick, taken a drink of water because the sickness made them powerfully thirsty, and died.

"My son?" Captain Truckee's was voice tight.

Sarah's own heart froze. Was her father one of those who had died?

But the messenger quickly assured them Chief Winnemucca was alive. The California party cantered sadly into camp. Sarah's father, his broad shoulders bowed with grief, came forward to meet his father.

"It was the river," Winnemucca told his father. "It must have been poisoned by the white settlers. Poison water killed our people. We should take revenge on the whites!"

Sarah's grandfather pulled away, his face

angry. "I cannot believe my white brothers would do such a thing. If they had poisoned the river, they, too, would have died when they drank the water. It must have been some fearful disease unknown to us."

Sarah, listening quietly, remembered that the medicine man had once said that sickness would kill more of their people than white man's bullets.

"They are on our land," Winnemucca stated flatly. "More citizens come every day and take our hunting grounds."

In addition to the immigrants living along the river, there was a camp of soldiers sent to keep peace among the People and the whites. Although both the settlers and the soldiers were white, the People called the farmers and ranchers "citizens." The white people had their own term for the People: "Paiutes."

"Yes," Captain Truckee agreed. "They are already here in our land. We must let our brothers live with us. We cannot just tell them to go away. If we fight them, we will lose. It would be a mistake to make war on the whites. More good people would die."

They mourned the dead. Sarah joined her relatives in the ritual of cutting off hair and crying for the loved ones. After they had prayed, Captain Truckee held up his paper-friend.

"Does this paper look as if it could talk and ask for anything?" he said. "Yet it does. It can ask for something for us to eat. I will take my paper-friend down to the white soldiers and ask for sacks of flour."

He took Winnemucca and some other men down to the soldier-camp. When they came back, they carried sacks of flour. Sarah's father wore a new red shirt and had a red blanket slung over one shoulder. He would not take revenge on the white men now.

It would not be easy to forget the friends and loved ones who had died, probably from a disease the white men brought with them. But they would try and get along with the white men. Warfare would only lead to more deaths. This was the only way the People could survive.

Seasons passed. Sarah traveled with her people from the summer hunting grounds to the pine-nut forests in the mountains. She grew from an inquisitive little girl into a bright young woman. Her face was pleasingly round, with smooth, honey-colored skin. Her sturdy figure hinted of female curves to come.

Sarah was old enough to go charm the antelope. Her father allowed women and young people on the expedition, but no small children.

When they were all assembled at the special meeting place, the chief chose two men to be his messengers to the antelope. With one moccasin-pointed toe, Winnemucca sketched a circle in the dirt. The People began constructing wickiups along the circle. No lodges were built in the center of the side facing sunrise. Beyond this gap, the antelope herd peacefully grazed.

After the lodges were finished, they gathered sagebrush. Sarah helped stack brush into six high mounds, which created a barrier between the grazing herd and their camp. She moved slowly, careful not to stumble. No one could trip or accidently drop a piece of brush. If anyone fumbled, he was supposed to tell the chief and they would start over.

When the morning star hung low in the sky, Sarah sat with her father and the others in the opening of the lodge-circle. Winnemucca lit his pipe and passed it to the right. Then the chief took out a deerhide drum. Sarah had never seen it before. The People made no music of any kind. This drum was only used for charming antelope. With a stick, her father rubbed the taut skin sides, making a strange vibrating sound.

Now the two antelope messengers walked across the camp to the opening, then crossed and separated. They circled the herd in opposite directions, not letting the antelope see them.

In the evening, the People sat in the opening and smoked the pipe. Again, the chief played his drum. Although her father had the gift, Sarah knew he needed the help of his people to charm the antelope.

The next day everyone in the tribe circled the antelope with the messengers, weaving the spell around the creatures. The ritual was repeated every day for five days.

On the fifth day, the antelope meekly followed the tracks of the People into the mound-circle. Some tossed their heads, but most looked sleepy, enchanted. Inside the mound-circle, they ran around as if fenced in. But there was no fence. The People had made them believe the animals were trapped, which in fact they were not. If any one of the People had stumbled or dropped a piece of brush during the constructing of the mounds, the spell would not have worked and the antelope would have fled through the opening like flood-water rushing through a canyon.

But no one had made any mistakes and the charm worked in perfect order. Eventually the antelope calmed down and the men moved in for the kill. There would be a good supply of meat that winter.

Sarah took her place alongside the other women to dress the meat. The ritual was interesting but this part was not. The women always prepared the game and skinned the hides, just as they always tended the cook-fires and minded the little ones.

Sarah wished she could do something different. She did not look forward to a life of grinding pine nuts and stitching moccasins. Yet what other life was there?

One spring morning, she stepped out of her wickiup. She prayed to *Thuwipu Unipugant*, One Who Made the Earth, and cast some ashes east, asking the sun to banish any bad dreams she'd had that night and make her day a good one. Then she sniffed the sweet air and knew instinctively that the flower she had been named for was finally in bloom.

"My flower is blooming!" she said joyfully.

All the girls Sarah's age chattered excitedly as they went about their morning chores. Their mothers understood — they had once been young themselves — and let their daughters finish early. The girls ran giggling into the hills. Sarah picked handfuls of the delicate-petaled shell-flower she had been named for.

Other girls exclaimed when they saw "themselves" in bloom. They laughed and talked as if they were the flowers they had been named for. It was such fun!

When they returned to camp, the chief made an announcement.

"My daughters," he said. "I am told that you have seen your name-flowers in the hills and valleys. Five days from today your festival day will come."

Young men eyed the girls, excitement leaping in their dark eyes. At the Flower Festival, a young man could sing and dance with a special girl.

Sarah spent the next five days preparing for the festival. She collected armloads of shell-flowers, weaving them into garlands and crowns. As she worked, she hummed her flower song.

On the day of the festival, the Flower Girls came marching out, singing their flower songs, and wearing wreaths of flowers.

Sarah sang:

"My name is Thoc-me-tony, the shell-flower. I am so beautiful! Who will come and dance with me? Come and be happy with me! I shall be beautiful while the earth lasts . . . "

As she danced, she was no longer Sarah, the young Numa girl, but Thoc-me-tony, the shell-flower. She was as beautiful as a new day, as light and carefree as the spring breeze.

A young man danced beside her. The boy's name was Winnenap. She had noticed him glancing at her at the river whenever she went for water. Of course she always cast her glance downward as she had been taught and he never spoke to her because he was not a male relative. But she was glad he was dancing with her.

All day the young people sang and danced. Then they returned to camp, where their parents welcomed them with a special feast. The festival was over.

Sarah was no longer a girl. Her family treated her as a woman now.

6

"**Y**ou don't sit on the floor," Sarah instructed her younger sister, Elma. "You sit in the *chair*."

Elma looked at the table and chairs with the same awe Sarah had experienced many summers ago, when they had gone into the white man's house in California. The memory of the beautiful red chair had stayed with Sarah all those seasons.

Now Sarah was twelve summers. Elma was three summers younger. They were in the home of Major William Ormsby, in Genoa, on Lake Tahoe. Major Ormsby was Captain Truckee's great friend. Captain Truckee had asked the major if his two granddaughters could live with the major's family to learn the language and ways of his white brothers. The major agreed.

Although Sarah loved her grandfather, she wished he had asked her if she wanted to go live with strange white people. But she knew she had to do as he told her to. Already she chafed at the confining role of a Numa woman. At least at Major Ormsby's, she would be able to learn new things.

Sarah and Elma made the journey south on horseback to the deep, blue lake cradled in the mountains. The water of Lake Tahoe was as glassy as obsidian, the volcanic stone the People used to make arrowheads, and reflected the tall pine trees.

The town of Genoa was populated by soldiers and Mormons, white men who practiced a different type of religion.

The Ormsby house wasn't as tall as the house of red stone in Stockton that Sarah remembered so well, but it had many beautiful things to look at inside. Sarah was especially enchanted with the paintings hanging on the walls, scenes of cool rivers shaded by leafy green trees and likenesses of white ladies wearing gowns of silk and satin.

Margaret Ormsby, the major's wife, wore a dress of moss-green silk when she welcomed Sarah and Elma to her home. Sarah admired the garment's softness.

"It is like spiderwebs," she said, struggling to find the English words. She remembered a little from her year in California, but here she would learn to speak English better.

Margaret Ormsby laughed. "That's exactly what silk *is* made from, the cocoons of special spiders."

Sarah warmed to the major's wife. She was very pretty, with a round face like Sarah's, blue eyes, and brown hair soft as a badger's pelt. She wore her hair swept back from a center part and gathered in a knot on the back of her neck. Sarah decided when her hair grew out again, she would wear hers the same way.

The major, a tall, thin man, had short chin whiskers and light-colored blue eyes. He greeted Captain Truckee's granddaughters, adding he hoped they would be happy in his home.

Mrs. Ormsby showed them around the house. Sarah pointed out — in English — the articles of furniture she remembered from her stay in California. Elma had been too young to remember that trip. In addition to warning her sister not to sit on the floor when they ate, Sarah cautioned her not to touch the white people's things unless she was invited to do so.

"You speak some English already," Mrs. Ormsby observed.

"Yes," Sarah said. "I learned a little when my grandfather took us to California. And my grandfather has taught me what he knows." To further impress the major's wife, Sarah began singing "The Star-Spangled Banner."

Mrs. Ormsby laughed again. Sarah loved the sound of the woman's laughter — it was like water running over round stones.

"You sing very well, Sarah. Perhaps you will

sing for my guests sometime. We don't have fancy parties here, but we do like to get together for socials."

Mrs. Ormsby showed them where they would sleep, in a little room just off the kitchen. Sarah put her hand tentatively on the cot she would share with Elma. They had never slept on a white man's bed before. It would feel very strange.

Then Mrs. Ormsby gave them each a calico dress and a pair of boots. If they were to learn the ways of white people, they would have to dress like white girls.

Sarah eagerly stripped off her antelope skin garment. Because it was summer, she wore yucca sandals on her feet instead of her hide moccasins. She slipped the soft, cool calico over her head, marveling at the lightness of the fabric. Then she twirled, making the skirt flare.

"You look beautiful," Elma told her. "How do you fasten these little round things?" Sarah helped her sister with the slippery bone buttons.

They both loved their dresses, but were not as delighted with the boots. The boots did not fit and pinched their toes.

"I want to wear my sandals," Elma said.

Sarah frowned. "You cannot. We have to dress like the white ladies while we are here."

Elma limped around the room. "No wonder the white ladies walk with such tiny steps. Their feet hurt them!"

"Well, if the white women do not mind cramped toes, then neither will we."

"But we are not white women," Elma said.

"No," Sarah agreed. "But Grandfather wants us to learn their ways and we will."

"We have to work, too," Elma reminded her.

"Work never hurt anyone." Sarah was certain that preparing meals in the Ormsby house would be more interesting than making pine-nut mush.

Mrs. Ormsby, like most white people, could not pronounce Thoc-me-tony. "I will call you Sarah and you Elma," she told the girls. It was the way of the whites to give the Paiutes new names.

Sarah liked the light, airy sound of her white name, but inside, she was still Thoc-me-tony.

Margaret Ormsby patiently taught them how to prepare coffee, the hot black water white people seemed to drink all day, how to set the table with plates and eating implements, how to fry an egg. Sarah was amazed that Mrs. Ormsby did not stoop over a cook-fire to prepare meals. She stood at a black iron box that had a fire burning its belly and she cooked on its hot surface.

Sarah enjoyed sewing. With practice, her seams were as fine as Margaret Ormsby's. Her English vocabulary grew each day. She also picked up Spanish from the Mexicans who traveled the Old California Trail.

"You have an ear for languages," Mrs. Ormsby

praised Sarah one day. "It is a real talent and I hope you make use of it. Helping people understand one another is very important, especially out here."

Sarah loved lesson-time, when they sat around the table after supper with Mrs. Ormsby's worn schoolbooks. Margaret taught the girls history and figuring. Elma was not as keen to learn as her sister. Sarah could not get enough.

When Mrs. Ormsby taught Sarah the alphabet, Sarah sensed all the secrets of the world were about to be revealed to her. The key to gaining knowledge, she realized, was learning to read and write. Sarah's proudest moment came when she was able to spell her name in clumsy letters. Now she could talk on paper! When she returned to the People, she would show her grandfather she could talk to his paper-friend.

Sarah learned to tell the hour with the white man's time-keeping device, the clock, instead of the sun, and to mark the passage of time using a calendar, instead of the seasons. She became accustomed to her pleasant life with the Ormsbys. She sometimes missed her parents and grandfather, but did not talk about returning to them.

The months sped by. Sarah turned thirteen. Soon she and Elma had been living in Genoa a year. They had no idea trouble was brewing between their people and the whites until one sunny

September morning when their brother Natchez and their cousin Numaga rode up to the Ormsby house.

Sarah was surprised that Major Ormsby had sent for them. She stood anxiously on the porch, in case she was needed to interpret. Major Ormsby asked Natchez to translate. Sarah hid her anger. She spoke English better than her brother, but because he was a man, *he* was chosen for the job.

"Whose arrows are these?" the major demanded, as soon as Natchez and Numaga dismounted. "These are the arrows that murdered two white men. I want to know what tribe these arrows belong to."

Numaga, who was war chief, examined the arrows. "They belong to the Washoes."

"I want you to ask the Washoe chief to turn over the men who shot these arrows," the major ordered. "Or we will make war on them. Tell him that."

The Numa had signed a treaty with the whites. As long as they cooperated with the soldiers, they would be protected. But they had to do as the army commanded.

That night the peace-loving People performed the first war dance Sarah had ever witnessed. Her heart skipped at the sight of painted faces, eerie and frightening in the leaping firelight. Was that sinister figure her brother? Could that monster be her kindly uncle? The incident of the Washoe arrows had forced her people to become warlike.

Sarah felt anger mixed with frustration. If the People refused to honor the treaty — which they would never do — they would lose the protection of the soldiers. But if they did as the army ordered, they might be killed in a war with the Washoes. There was no way the Numa could win.

The next day, Captain Jim, the chief of the Washoes, was brought before Major Ormsby. Resplendent in his robe and necklace of bones, the Washoe chief soberly admitted the arrows belonged to his people. "But no Washoe killed the white men," he said.

"There are two guilty Washoe warriors and they will have to be brought in for trial," the major insisted. "If not, the Paiutes will make war on the Washoes, because the Paiutes are friends with the whites."

Terrified that his tribe would be massacred by the powerful white soldiers, Captain Jim surrendered three of his men. Numaga and Natchez had promised Captain Jim that the men would be tried in California, according to white man's law.

But the men were never tried. They broke free and, attempting to escape, were shot by white settlers. The wives of the dead men screamed. Sarah heard one woman moan over and over that her husband was innocent. Sarah knew the Washoe woman was speaking the truth. Innocent men had died for a crime they did not commit.

The truth eventually came out. Two white men had killed their own white brothers for money, then placed Washoe arrows in the wounds to cover their crime. The incident opened another wound between the People and the whites. The treaty had been broken as if it were a pine-nut shell, promises scattered to the wind like so much dust.

With the tense situation between the People and whites, Sarah and her sister could no longer stay at the Ormsbys'. Sarah took off her calico dress and found her antelope skins.

"When we go home, do we act like white ladies?" Elma wanted to know, slipping off her dress.

"No," Sarah replied. "There is no place for fancy manners in our camp."

"Why have we learned the ways of the whites if we are to forget them?"

"We will not forget," Sarah said. "But we are not white women. We are the daughters of a chief and it is time to return to our people."

Because the weather was cooler, Sarah put on her moccasins. Her feet remembered the feel of the soft skins. She could walk easier.

Proudly she walked out of the major's house, no longer an Indian girl pretending to be a white person. She was going back to the Numa, where she belonged.

7

Shunning the white man's calendar, Sarah went back to the Numa way of marking the passage of time by seasons: the time of the *taboose*, the jumping of the lake trout, the time of the sagebrush blooming.

Sage was a hardy plant that grew abundantly, a wide gray sea rolling from shore to shore of the Great Basin. The brush provided shelter and fuel — a sagebrush cook-fire was very hot.

The People were much like the sturdy sagebrush, Sarah thought, gazing out at the life-giving bushes marching down the hill from her *karnee*. Tenacious, able to adapt to all weathers, and blessed with the ability to find nourishment in a harsh, pitiless land. The land was their home, the winds, the mountains, the pine forests. They did not build houses like the whites and stay in one place. The Numa moved with the seasons.

We live here because we *can*, Sarah thought one day after she had returned from Major Orms-

59

by's. At first it was difficult to go back to the old way of life, cooking over fires instead of stoves, trudging down to the lake for water instead of drawing a bucket from a convenient well.

But after a while the white man's ways seemed unnecessarily cumbersome, like all the implements required for the simple act of eating. The Indian ate from a flat basket, using a spoon from the horn of a bighorn sheep. The white man ate with knives, forks, spoons, with plates, bowls, cups, glasses.

Life would be easier in other places, like California, Sarah knew, but the People would not be free there. They would have to share the land with whites, Mexicans, and other Indians. The People could only be themselves in this ocean of silvery-green bounded by rugged mountains.

But that life was rapidly changing.

In the two sagebrush seasons since Sarah had left Genoa to return to her people, hundreds of white immigrants poured into Washoe, as they named the Nevada territory west of the Santa Rosa range. Many were on their way to California. "Forty-niners," they were called, men with gold fever. But many also stayed, camping along the banks of the Humboldt and Carson rivers.

Mormons, white men seeking religious freedom, treated the People the kindliest. Although they settled on the People's land, the Mormons learned the language of the Numa so they could communicate. They enlisted the aid of the People to help them build houses, fences, and irrigation ditches. Several of Sarah's distant cousins had helped Mormons prepare fields for crops.

But as those early crude camps grew into large permanent colonies, the Mormons didn't need the Indians' help. Other white settlers came and took more land to graze thousands of heads of cattle. They felled vast stands of pine-nut trees for fences, firewood, and lumber.

Without their land to support them, and without the food and supplies earned from working for the settlers, the People began to starve. They had no place to live and no way to feed their families. Strange sicknesses plagued them — red spots, high fevers, swollen jaws. The medicine man of Sarah's tribe said they were catching white man's illnesses, carried downstream from the white settlements or borne on the wind. His prayers were to no avail. Many People died from disease.

And then, when it seemed the situation between whites and the People could get no worse, silver was discovered in Washoe.

The forty-niners, in their hurry to strike it rich, were only interested in crossing the Great Basin as a way to get to the goldfields of California. They often shot the People for sport, contemptuously calling them "Diggers." To the miners, "Digger

Indians" were the lowest form of life. They wrongly accused the People of thievery and scorned them for eating lizards.

Sarah blazed with anger at this shameful treatment. Who was to say the miners were more civilized than the People? If being civilized meant shooting innocent men and women for sport, then she would gladly stay savage. But at least these terrible men were only passing through.

Some determined prospectors chased rumors of gold in the pine-nut forests. All they found, to their disgust, were flakes of the precious yellow metal in heavy black mud, too little gold to be worth anyone's effort. But then a prospector had the black mud assayed and learned it was rich in silver.

At first Sarah did not understand the white man's obsession with the bright substance, but soon realized what the discovery meant to her people.

Overnight, the flood of miners heading for California changed their course for Washoe. Hordes of silver-seekers poured into the Great Basin: Mexicans driving trains of mules, eastern gentlemen on fancy thoroughbreds, grizzled prospectors leading strings of pack ponies — all came to make their fortune in silver.

The new settlers and prospectors ignored the treaty made between the whites and the People. The People had no protection against the miners who used them as slave labor or shot them for no reason.

The peaceful world that had existed between sagebrush and sky was no more. Sarah realized the old way of life was over. She did not think her people knew what she did — that their time was past.

That fall, Sarah's tribe ventured into the mountains to gather pine nuts as usual. Her grandfather led the expedition, following the ancient trails, but Sarah sensed his heart was heavy. He wanted desperately for his people to get along with his white brothers.

"It is the only way," he kept saying. "We will not survive unless we learn to live together in peace."

But the tensions between the People and the whites increased with each setting sun. Sarah often thought of the story about the four children, two dark and two light, and how they were banished from the land once before because they had quarreled. Now the white brothers had returned, but not to begin healing the old trouble. They came for their own selfish reasons.

The tribe journeyed far into the pine-nut mountains. Entire groves had been ruthlessly chopped down for firewood and lumber. The whites did not care that they were destroying the People's most important food source.

The higher the Numa climbed, the colder it became. Down below, the days were breathlessly hot. Here, the hard, bright sun burned through the *pogonip*, the chilly morning fog that shrouded the mountains with an opaque veil. Frost crystals preserved the hoofprints of mule deer. Blossoms of shooting stars sagged under a coating of ice. Up here in the dark, silent forests, it could snow any month of the year, even in summer.

Sarah walked steadily, breathing in clean, sharp air. If she climbed too quickly, the thinness of the air would make her head ache and her limbs feel heavy. As she walked behind Natchez, she gave silent thanks to *Numunana*, the People Father, for they were entering the Dwelling Place of a Great Spirit. There were lesser guardian powers in the steep rock walls, in the trees, in the animals that roamed the forests, even in the wind and weather. Careful not to offend any of the spirits, Sarah offered prayers to each for allowing the People to intrude.

They located a stand of trees thickly studded with pinecones, made camp and set to work. Men hunted for the scarce deer, driven into the deep woods by the white men's guns. Women strapped baskets on their backs and gathered pinecones.

Later, Sarah wondered if she had left out a guardian spirit or if her prayer had somehow offended one. Then she wondered if her grandfather had been too worried about his white brothers and his people to notice where he was stepping. Sarah could not blame the whites for making her grandfather careless, but the accident might not have happened if her grandfather had not been so burdened with problems.

Captain Truckee did not see the poisonous snake until the snake had coiled and struck just behind his knee. He fell with a cry. Sarah's father ran forward to catch him. Winnemucca carried his father back to the camp, summoning Puagant, the medicine man.

The medicine man gave Captain Truckee some hot water to drink and chanted a healing song. The captain roused a bit and demanded that he be taken back down into the valley. The men swiftly built a litter to carry him. The tribe hiked back down the mountain, reaching their base camp by nightfall.

Inside the Winnemucca lodge, the medicine man continued his healing ritual long into the night. Putting smooth polished stones from his medicine pouch into his mouth, he began singing. From her pallet, Sarah heard the chant, "Nani, nani, nani, naaaani," loudly, then softly. She saw Puagant bend over her grandfather's knee, which was pillowed on hides, and spit out one of the stones. He then picked up the stone and crawled outside the *karnee* to bury the evil spirit that flew out with the stone.

In the morning Captain Truckee was a little

better. He let Sarah feed him some pine-nut mush. But by afternoon, his fever rose, as if with the journey of the sun.

"I am going to die," he told Sarah weakly. "Will you ask your dear father to send for my white brother Mr. Snyder? I wish to see him before I go to the Spirit-Land."

Sarah was alarmed, but she relayed the message to her father. Mr. Snyder was one of Captain Truckee's friends. When Mr. Snyder saw the chief was obviously dying, he was clearly disturbed.

"You'll get well, my friend," he said.

Truckee waved one feeble hand. "You see there are my two little girls and there is my big girl, and there are my two boys. They are my son's children, my grandchildren. The two young girls I want you to take to California, to my friend Mr. Scott. They will send them to the sisters' school in San Jose. This is my last request. Will you promise to do this for me?"

Snyder took Captain Truckee's hand and squeezed it. "I promise."

"Then it is good-bye, my friend," Truckee said. "Perhaps one day we will meet again in the Spirit-Land. Now I want to talk to my own people."

As the man left, Sarah glimpsed tears in his eyes. Her grandfather had made many friends during his long life.

"You are now the head chief of our people," Truckee said to Winnemucca. In a halting whisper, he advised his son to be a good father to his people. Then he began to cry. All those gathered around his pallet cried also. Sarah could not believe her grandfather was dying. What would she do without him?

Signal fires smoked from every mountaintop, telling of the great chief's passing. People journeyed all that night to bid their chief farewell. Captain Truckee received visitors the next morning, but was unable to speak. Puagant laid his hands on the chief again, but to no avail. This time the captain did not rally. All that day and through most of the night, Sarah kept watch, listening to his ragged breathing. She did not sleep, afraid her grandfather would die while she slept.

When the seven stars reached the same place the sun reached at midday, Sarah's grandfather half-turned. Sarah thought this was a good sign. He was getting better!

But the medicine man said, "He is dying now. He will open his eyes soon."

The captain did open his eyes. He asked Sarah's father to raise him up so he could speak one last time.

"I'm so tired. I shall soon be happy. I hope you will live to see as much as I have, and to know as much as I do. Do your duty as I have done to your people and your white brothers."

He closed his eyes again. Sarah's mother thought he had died and began weeping.

"His spirit has not yet left his body," said Puagant.

With great effort, the chief continued, "Do not throw away my paper-friend. Place it on my breast when you bury me." His voice failed.

Puagant made a sharp gesture. "He has spoken his last words, he has given his last look. His spirit is leaving, he will speak once as he enters the Spirit-Land."

Sarah drew closer to his pallet. Her grandfather's lips moved as if he were whispering. Then he was still.

She could not accept that her beloved grandfather would never speak to her again. She took his face in her hands, tears coursing down her cheeks, and gazed upon him, memorizing every line, the shape of his nose. The world grew dark around her. She was not aware of anyone else. No one mattered, only her grandfather. A great light had gone out.

Captain Truckee's body was kept in the wickiup for two days. Then he was buried in his rabbit-skin robes with all his possessions. Out of respect for the passing of a great chief, six of his horses were killed. The paper-friend was placed across his breast, as he had requested. No one would ever know exactly what the paper said. Although Sarah could make out letters a little, she could not read well enough to understand the document. She believed her grandfather's precious paper stated the simple truth: that he was a great man.

At the burial, the world seemed to close in around her. She could not surface from her grief. She thought about her grandfather's devotion to his white brothers. Her grandfather had wanted the whites and the People to live peacefully side-by-side. Sarah knew this would not be achieved easily, if ever.

Then she thought about the paper-friend. Above all, her grandfather had prized the ability to read. She saw a glimmer of light ahead.

She was going to school, where she would learn to talk on paper properly. It was her grandfather's dying wish.

But she wanted to learn for herself, as well. She had glimpsed the secrets of the world within Mrs. Ormsby's books and desired to know more. Armed with knowledge instead of a rifle or bow and arrow, she could help her people.

8

The winter after her grandfather died was the coldest in Sarah's memory. The People migrated into the mountains west of Humboldt Lake. They built their usual winter lodges of tightly-woven cattails and willow, insulated with sagebrush and ventilated with smoke holes.

But the early-winter blizzards that swept down from the Sierras soon buried their winter *karnees*. Snow drifted into the smoke holes, making it impossible to live in the lodges. The People retreated into caves, taking whatever food stores they could dig out of the snow.

The world was white and bitterly cold. In the mornings, the snow was frozen into glassy ridges. Sarah ventured out to chip ice to melt for water. Midday, the sky was often a blue so bright it hurt her eyes. But that beautiful sky soon clouded over, signaling the approach of yet another winter storm.

Besides suffering from the cold, the People did

not have enough to eat. Their autumn pine-nut harvest had been cut short by Captain Truckee's death. Cattle roamed over their land, grazing on grass which provided seeds, so there was little flour among the tribe. White men camped along the riverbanks, scaring off game. The unrest between whites and the People made regular food-gathering expeditions dangerous.

"The whites do not care if we starve," Sarah said bitterly. "Let us try to go hunting and they shoot us."

Bundled in rabbit-skin robes, she and her family shivered in their damp, cold cave, heated only by a small smoking fire. They shared what little food they had and waited for spring.

When at last the snows melted and valleys below began to bloom with spring flowers, the People left the mountain. Now Sarah and Elma could leave for the sisters' school in California.

Mr. Snyder came for them one April morning. Natchez and five other men were also accompanying the girls. They mounted up. Sarah was excited to be going to California once again. More than anything, she wanted to learn. Her horse pranced with high spirits along the Carson River, where pale green willows swayed gently over the water. But they soon met difficulties on the trail.

At the head of the river, they had to walk through a narrow, steep-walled canyon, leading their skittish ponies. The pass over the Sierras was open, but winter still gripped the land. On a good day in high summer Sarah knew the journey required six sleeps to make it over the pass. At times the trail was blocked by drifts. Every morning, ice frosted their robes, but as they left the snow line above them, the days became warmer, though the rugged road was not any easier. The Sierras seemed to be nothing but snow and rocks. They were forced to lead their ponies through most of the Sierra crossing.

And then they were in California, where they traded their horses for a ticket on a stagecoach. Because the stage lines did not allow Indians to ride inside the coaches, Sarah and the others rode on top, joggling with the luggage. Mr. Snyder, of course, had a seat inside. Sarah was too engrossed with the passing sights to mind where she sat.

A Pony Express rider pulled alongside the coach for a brief time. The leather pouch he carried contained paper-friends such as her grandfather had had, Sarah knew. The horse's hooves pounded furiously, churning up great clouds of dust. The stagecoach driver told her that the rider would exchange his weary horse for a fresh one at the next station.

In Sacramento, they said good-bye to Mr. Snyder. Captain Truckee's friend Mr. Scott would escort them the rest of the way to San Jose. When they rode a steamboat down the river, Sarah thought the steamboat was very tired, as it made panting sounds downstream. Mr. Scott told her the puffing noise was steam, which fueled the engine and made the steamboat run. Sarah clung to the rail, amazed by the white man's abilities.

The steamboat carried them all the way to San Francisco. Sarah and Elma stared at the vast number of white men's lodges rambling up the steep hills. They visited a market on the waterfront. Sarah had never seen so much fish in her entire life.

"Surely the rivers and streams are emptied of fish!" she said. But Mr. Scott assured her the market was stocked with this much fish and more, each and every day.

White men did not allow Indians to sleep in their overnight lodges, so she and her companions camped outside. Sarah did not think this was fair treatment. If the Indian had money to pay for a room, he should be allowed inside the hotel, just as he should be allowed inside the stagecoach.

They rode another steamboat down the San Francisco Bay to Santa Clara. From there, it was only a short journey south to San Jose.

The mission was a large brick building with a cross-tipped steeple. A canal flowed lazily past the mission. The Sisters of Notre Dame de Namur had established the school.

The new students were quickly admitted. Mother Superior remembered meeting Captain Truckee and recalled her promise to teach his granddaughters when they became old enough. She was delighted to honor the request of the distinguished chief.

Mr. Scott thanked Mother Superior and left. Natchez bade his sisters farewell.

A nun in a beautiful black robe greeted the girls. "My name is Sister Catherine," she said. Sarah much admired the beads the nun wore. "This is my rosary," the sister told her. "I use it in prayer."

"Ah!" Sarah nodded. "A type of chanting string."

"You speak English quite well," Sister Catherine commented.

She showed Sarah and Elma the dormitory upstairs. Cloud-sheer curtains billowed at the windows, which overlooked the desert that rolled toward distant brown mountains.

Four beds occupied the sunny room. Sarah and Elma each had their own iron cot. Having a bed of her own was an unbelievable luxury, Sarah thought. The other two beds belonged to their roommates, whom they would meet later.

Sister Catherine brought them clothes and showed them how to wash up. Sarah and Elma were familiar with the white man's hygiene — Mrs. Ormsby had insisted they wash up at the kitchen pitcher and basin daily. Again, the nun seemed pleasantly surprised.

"She thinks we are savages," Elma told Sarah

as they changed from their buckskin garb into calico dresses.

"We are the daughters and granddaughters of chiefs," Sarah said. "We must not forget that."

When they were dressed, a girl their age came into the room. Sarah stared at her, entranced by her beauty. The girl was as slender as a willow sapling, with glossy black hair and huge dark eyes under brows like ravens' wings.

She spoke English with a lilting accent. "I am Martina. I also share this room. Our other roommate is Luz — you will see her later. I have come to take you down to your lesson."

As they walked downstairs into the cool flagstone hall, Sarah introduced herself and her sister. Martina was impressed that they were the daughters of chiefs.

"You are Indian princesses!" she exclaimed, then curtseyed gracefully. Her dark eyes shone with merriment as she giggled.

Sarah laughed, too. Martina was an amusing girl. She was glad to have made a friend so quickly in her new school.

Martina led them into a bright, sparsely furnished room off the main corridor. Plain wooden benches stood in orderly ranks. Demure girls sat in pairs, a textbook across their aproned laps, listening to the nun at the front of the room.

Acknowledging the newcomers with a nod, the sister indicated an empty bench. Sarah and Elma sat down. The sister gave them a grammar text to share.

Taking a deep breath, Sarah looked down at the open book. For an instant, she was filled with panic. The symbols made no sense! Then the letters slowly formed themselves into words. Sarah was relieved; she had not forgotten what Margaret Ormsby had taught her. Folding her hands, she listened intently to what the nun was saying. She was determined to learn all she could.

After the grammar lesson was vocal music. Elma had a lovely singing voice. She knew lots of songs from their stay at the Ormsbys'. Both girls were fascinated with the organ Sister Margaret played.

The next lesson was religious instruction and Sarah read stories in the Bible. Although she did not abandon her belief in the Spirit Father, she accepted the white man's God, feeling that there was room for both deities in her soul.

After lessons, the girls went back to their room to get ready for supper. Martina chattered about the nuns.

A tall girl was arranging her heavy black hair with tortoiseshell combs when they walked in.

"There is an odor in this room," the girl said sullenly. "It smells like an animal carcass."

"This is Luz," Martina said to Sarah. "Luz, these are the new girls, Sarah and Elma."

Luz did not return Sarah's greeting or inquire

about her health or even remark upon the weather. She made none of the polite overtures the People made before entering a conversation.

Luz said only, "What is that smell?"

Embarrassed, Sarah retrieved the buckskin dresses from under her and Elma's beds. "I believe this is the source of the smell. I will remove our belongings if they offend you."

Martina turned on the other girl. "Luz, Sarah and Elma are the daughters of chiefs. You have insulted them."

Luz patted her hair smoothly over her ears. "I don't care if they are members of the crowned heads of Europe. Those animal hides stink."

Martina went with Sarah to dispose of the buckskins. "Pay no attention to Luz. She is jealous over my friendship with you. She has no friends in the school but me."

Sarah was alarmed. "I do not wish to cause trouble between you and your friend. If necessary, Elma and I will ask Sister Catherine to let us sleep in another room."

Martina waved her hand dismissively. "Luz is an old stick. You and your sister are the most exciting thing to happen in this school in ages. Don't fret about Luz."

There were too many delightful new experiences to sample without worrying about a grumpy roommate. Within a day, the chiefs' daughters eased into the routine of the school. They ate their meals in the dining hall, laughing with the other girls. The food was plentiful and tasty. Sarah's figure rounded into soft curves. She slept peacefully on smooth clean sheets and did not have disturbing dreams. They had lessons in grammar, history, geography, music, handwriting, and, Sarah's favorite, needlework.

Since her stay at the Ormsbys', she had loved sewing. Sister Catherine taught her coral work, worsted, darning, and embroidery, the making of beautiful pictures with threads. Sarah began a sampler, combining her skill in reading, writing, and needlework. On linen fabric, she stitched a quote from the Bible: "Blessed are the peacemakers, for they shall be called sons of God." The saying reminded her of her grandfather. He was a true peacemaker.

Sister Catherine singled out Sarah's work in class one morning, praising her neat hemstitch. Then she frowned as she examined Luz's work.

"Your French knots are too loose," the sister said. "Do them over."

Scowling, Luz picked out the sloppy stitches. "The Indian princess can do no wrong," she muttered, loud enough for Sarah to hear.

Sarah flushed, but said nothing. It was wisest to give the disagreeable girl a wide berth.

After class she went into the garden, where Mexican women tended the mission's vegetables. She worked on her sampler in the dry heat of the day, her head bent over her hoop, her fingers deftly pulling scarlet threads through the linen.

Within a few weeks, her English improved. She could talk on paper. At night in her room, she read the Bible by candlelight, following the closely lined print with her forefinger. She spoke Spanish with Martina and the Mexican women who did the laundry and prepared their meals.

Sarah was never happier. Like water seeping into sand, she soaked up knowledge. And she greatly admired the sisters. They knew everything and were so kind. Sarah decided that she wanted to be a teacher. There seemed no more honorable calling in the world than to fill young minds with knowledge.

Sometimes she wondered how her people were faring. They seemed very far away. Once Sarah guiltily caught herself thinking she never wanted to go back. If only she could learn and study with the nuns forever.

One morning, Sarah and Elma were summoned to Mother Superior. Sarah nervously checked her appearance in the mirror that hung over the washstand. She was clean and neat. In fact, just yesterday she had been awarded a shiny gold medal for "ladylike deportment." Sarah was proud of the medal and pinned it to the bodice of her dress.

"Have we done anything wrong?" Elma whispered to Sarah as they waited for Mother Superior to see them.

Sarah shook her head. She could not think of anything. They got along well with the sisters and the other students. Only Luz did not like them, but Sarah and Elma avoided the girl whenever possible. They had not made any trouble.

At last Sister Mary ushered them into Mother Superior's office. Mother Superior grasped their hands warmly, then came directly to the point.

"I am very sorry but you girls will have to leave our school," she said. "Apparently, one of our students told her parents about you. The parents object to having Indian girls studying with their daughters. If it were up to me, I would allow them to remove *their* daughter. Unfortunately, this school depends on the support of those parents and others. So you will have to go. I will send for Mr. Scott to take you away."

Sarah blinked as sudden tears welled. Leave the sisters' school! She had come to love the mission dearly. Now she would have to return to her people, all because one girl's mother and father did not believe Sarah was good enough to be in the same school as their daughter. Not good enough! Did she not have a medal to prove she was ladylike? But Sarah swallowed her argument. It was not Mother Superior's fault.

Martina helped them to pack. "It was that Luz," she snapped. "She tattled to her father. I would rather have a whole school full of girls like you than Luz. I wish *she* were leaving!"

The sisters let Sarah and Elma keep their clothes and Sarah was permitted to take her embroidery hoop and silks. Hugging Sister Catherine, she promised to finish her sampler.

As they walked through the mission gates, Sarah looked back. Her heart was heavy under the gold medal pinned to her dress.

Martina waved good-bye. "One day you will come back!"

Sarah hoped so. Her grandfather's dying wish had been that she acquire an education. She was determined to continue her schooling to make his dream come true.

And she had a dream of her own. Someday she would be a teacher herself. She would put the key of knowledge into the hands of her people, so they would know the secrets of the world.

9

The girls stayed at Mr. Scott's house for one week, waiting for Natchez to come and take them home.

"Your brother can't come and get you." Then Mr. Scott told Sarah, "There's some trouble back home. He sent word to put you and your sister on a stagecoach. Can you travel by yourselves?"

"Yes, we will be fine," Sarah replied, wondering what trouble was preventing her brother from escorting them back.

Mr. Scott drove them to the Overland station, wishing them a safe journey. He added he hoped the trouble — whatever it was — would be resolved peacefully. Sarah took his hand and shook it. Mr. Scott had been her grandfather's great friend. He understood the People better than most whites. She thanked him for his kindness and then climbed on top of the coach, where she and Elma sat among trunks and string-bound boxes.

The stage was running late. The driver's whip cracked and the six-horse team leaped forward, nearly dislodging Sarah from her perch among the tied-down luggage. Elma grabbed her wrist before she was pitched over the side.

The coach lurched over the trail, past the tidy farms of the Sacramento Valley and into the hilly ranch country. Yellow mustard and blue lupine were in full bloom. At midday, they stopped to water the horses at another Overland station. Sarah and Elma sat in the shade of the coach and ate the napkin-wrapped ham biscuits Mrs. Scott had packed for them.

That evening they stopped at a tavern, a ramshackle clapboard building in danger of falling down. Sarah and Elma were not permitted to take meals in the dining room, but the driver brought them out a plate. The other passengers slept in the inn's rooms while the girls camped out under the stars.

Early the next morning they were off again, tackling the mountains that rose between the valley and the Great Basin.

"Washoe Territory!" the driver bawled late that afternoon.

When Sarah saw the familiar sage-covered hills, she felt like a stranger. This was not the first time she had experienced this feeling of separateness. When she and Elma were staying at Major Ormsby's, Sarah adapted to the white man's world quite easily. She liked their clothes and chairs and the wonderful things they had. At the sisters' school, she enjoyed the serene days devoted to learning.

Yet she was not white. She was one of the People. It was difficult to switch back and forth between the two worlds.

As the coach jounced over the rutted, dusty road, she turned her attention to the problem Mr. Scott had mentioned. What was happening? How serious was the trouble?

She found out as soon as the stage dropped them off at Pyramid Lake. The lake sparkled deep blue in the afternoon sun. A large rock cut through the water, pointing toward the clear blue sky. Sarah breathed a sigh of relief. They were home.

But where was everyone? The People should have been out fishing. She saw no one on the sandy banks, spearing *cui-cui*, the huge, ugly trout. It was ominously still.

Then Natchez stepped out of a clump of brush. Numaga, the war chief, was with him. Both men looked grim. Natchez spoke the welcoming speech, but his eyes were hooded with weariness.

"I am sorry I could not come for you," he told Sarah. "You know I would not have let you travel alone."

"Yes, but Elma and I are all right," she reassured him. "What is happening?"

"There is a big council tonight. All the tribes of our people are at the lake, or are on their way."

"Why?" Sarah's heart quivered with fear. The far-flung tribes of the Numa did not often gather together. Something terrible must have happened for her father to call a meeting of all of his people.

"We will decide to make war on the whites."

Sarah stared wide-eyed at him. The Numa rarely made war on anyone! They were a peace-loving people, preferring to solve differences by negotiation. They would only be driven to fight if some terrible wrong had been made against them.

As they walked back to camp, Numaga explained what had happened.

"Two young girls went out digging roots. They did not come back, and so their parents went to search for them. They could not find their children. Our people followed their trail to the lodge of two white traders called Williams. The brothers said they had not seen the girls and let our people look in their cabin. We did not find the children." He paused. "It is our belief that the children are being held prisoner. A war party is gathering to take our children and kill the white men who hold them against their will."

"What are the soldiers saying?" Sarah asked. The treaty her father had signed obligated the army to peacefully solve disputes between the citizens and the People.

"You know what they are saying," her brother answered bitterly. "Major Ormsby will not even listen to us."

Sarah did not understand this. When she had stayed with the major, she received only kindness from him. But then she remembered how unreasonable the major had been over the incident of the Washoe arrows.

That night the men gathered around the council fire. The chiefs sat in an inner circle, passing the pipe. The warriors, many of them already painted for war, drew close to hear what was being said.

Sarah slipped from the shadows to the outer edge of the circle, where she would not be seen. Women were not permitted to take part in this council, but Sarah could not keep away. Whatever the decision, she would be affected — she had loyalties to both her own people and to her white brothers. The white man's religion, Christianity, decreed that all people love one another. The Numa held the same belief.

Firelight flickered on the chiefs' faces. The shifting shadows emphasized their serious expressions. Winnemucca sat importantly in the center. Sarah recognized Sa-a-ba, chief of the Smoke Creek Numa; Moguan-noga, leader of the Humboldt Meadows Numa; Nojomud, chief of the Honey Lake Numa; Se-quinta, leader of the People who lived at Black Rock. The medicine man of Antelope Valley was there, along with leaders of two other tribes — the Shoshone, whose land bordered that of the People, and the Bannocks, who lived to the north. Numaga sat on the right-hand of Winnemucca. From the mutterings made by men around her, Sarah gathered that the council members were divided on the question of going to war.

Numaga stood now to speak. "I have journeyed to California and seen the soldiers and cannon that will be sent to fight us. We are brave people, but I have seen the strength of the white men. They are like the stars in the sky, without number. We cannot win a war against the whites."

"You have red skin, but your heart is white," Chief Winnemucca said with contempt. "Why do you not go and live among the white brothers you love so much?"

Sarah bit her lip. Her father was not following the teachings of Captain Truckee. Her grandfather would be against a war with the whites, not for it. Yet she understood the frustration her father must be feeling.

"I have lain for three days, without food and water, without moving," Numaga said, "to show you how much I do not wish this war. Some of you have threatened me; others have listened to me. Our enemies are like the sands in the beds of our rivers; when taken away they only make place for more to come. Should we defeat the whites here, an army of white men from over the mountains in California will come and cover our country like a blanket."

There was a silence, then Numaga added, "I

love our people. Let us live. And when our spirits shall be called to the Great Camp in the southern sky, let our bones rest where our fathers are buried."

It was an eloquent speech. Tears stung Sarah's eyes. Surely her people would find some other way to settle this problem.

Just then a messenger thundered into the council circle, leaping off his still-running pony. He spoke to Chief Winnemucca. The chief stood and announced that the missing girls had been found hidden in a secret room under the floor of the Williams' cabin — bound, with rags stuffed in their mouths. Unspeakable things had been done to them.

Shouts of anger suddenly disrupted the council. Qu-da-zo-bo-eat, the Shoshone chief, gave an outraged cry.

Winnemucca added, "A number of my men, including my son Natchez, killed the white men and burned the cabin."

Sarah gasped. More than anything, her people believed in protecting their women. She realized that her brother and the others had no recourse other than to kill the white men and destroy their cabin. War was inevitable.

Numaga raised his hand to quiet the excited voices. "There is no further need for talk. All hope of peace is gone. The soldiers will come here to fight us. We must prepare for war."

The next day an army of white volunteers from nearby ranches and farms marched from Virginia City to Pyramid Lake. The warriors were waiting for them.

Sarah retreated to the mountains with the other women and children, where they would be safe. The entire day she waited at the entrance of the cave. She thought she would scream, not knowing what was happening. If only she could be in the battle. She could ride as well as any man and speak English better than anyone in her tribe. Her skills were being wasted in the caves.

That night Natchez came to see if the women were all right. Sarah immediately asked him what had happened.

"Your friend Major Ormsby did not realize the strength of the Numa," he said. "The white men ran like scalded coyotes!"

He went on to describe the clash of the two opposing forces near the lake. Ormsby's volunteers had seemed disorganized and ill-equipped, even for white men. Numaga rode forward to offer a truce, but Ormsby refused. Then Numaga organized his men to cleverly trap the whites. He sent out a few warriors, so it looked as if Numaga's army equaled Ormsby's troops in number. Ormsby signaled his men to gallop up the sandy slope. The white men moved almost at a leisurely pace. At the top, though, they met a surprise. Where it seemed no Indians could hide in the sagebrush and sand, hundreds rose up with a mighty cry.

The war cry unleashed great fear in the whites. They were not expecting the enemy to advance so fiercely. The People were not all armed with bows and arrows — many fired rifles, bought or traded from settlers like the Williams brothers. Frightened by the fury of the attack, Ormsby's volunteers raced their rearing horses back down the trail.

"Then the war is finished?" asked Elma.

Natchez shook his head. "Ormsby has asked us for the men who killed the Williams brothers. Our father will not do it."

Sarah put her hand on her brother's arm. Natchez had been one of the men present at the Williams' cabin the night of the killings. She knew Major Ormsby would not give up so easily after a humiliating defeat. He would demand that Natchez and any others involved be turned over to the army.

Major Ormsby sent for reinforcements. Blue coats marched steadily over the mountains from California, pulling their great cannons. More and more came, until they outnumbered Numaga's army like the stars in the sky he spoke of. But the People, embittered by endless grievances against the whites, would not surrender. White men had stolen their land, killed their game, and destroyed their food stores. Many had died at the hands of murderous whites. The People were angry and wanted revenge.

As spring turned to early summer, the Numa valiantly fought the blue-coated soldiers. The women lived on tule roots and prayed for the safety of their men.

Sarah learned that Major Ormsby had been killed. Natchez had tried to save the major's life when they met in battle. The major had lost his weapon and faced Natchez's rifle. Ormsby threw up his arms and begged Natchez not to kill him.

"I will fire over your head," Natchez had promised. "Drop down as if you are dead when I shoot."

The major did not understand and continued to plead for his life. Another warrior shot him dead.

Sarah was saddened by this news. She had been fond of Major Ormsby and wondered what would become of his wife, Margaret.

Natchez had other, more urgent news. The blue coats were bringing in reinforcements from California, led by a soldier-father more powerful than Major Ormsby. Numaga had ordered the women and children to flee to the north. Even here, in the foothills around Pyramid Lake, they were not free from danger.

Numaga's men, one thousand strong, were no match for the countless blue coats armed with cannons and more guns than trees in the pine-nut forest. Sarah, her sisters and mother fled safely to the northern mountains. Numaga managed to hold off the advancing troops so the women and children could escape. Then the force of the white man's army smothered his troops, like a huge basket upturned over a small fire. Bodies toppled into the lake and were washed ashore.

To save his people, Numaga and his men surrendered. From the top of a high mountain a white rag waved.

The war was over. The People had lost.

Soldiers drove the Numa from Pyramid Lake. Numaga, Winnemucca, and the other members of the Pyramid Lake tribe joined the women and children hiding in the mountains. They wandered the Black Rock Desert, an inhospitable alkali plain, longing for their home by the lake.

One night Natchez confided to Sarah, "Numaga was right. We lost what we loved because we fought the white men. We will never be able to go back."

Winnemucca overheard and nodded in agreement. "The bones of our ancestors lie in the mountain caves above the lake. We have lived there since the beginning of time. We have left our lake and now we will perish. The homesickness of an Indian is like death."

News filtered to the refugees that the white army was building a fort of stone and adobe on the Carson River. The soldiers would be able to hide inside and kill the People without ever leaving the shelter of the stone walls.

Numaga, anxious to know if this were the truth, went back to meet with the soldiers. There, he gave his word that the Numa would not make war on the whites for a year, *if* the white men also helped preserve peace. The commanding officer wanted Chief Winnemucca's presence to formalize the agreement.

Sarah and her family returned to Pyramid Lake. On the shores of their beloved lake, the Numa surrendered their weapons. The white soldier-father promised to protect them and give them their land back, but only under certain conditions. The Numa would receive food and supplies from the white man's government. They would learn to farm the land. The children would be taught to read and write. The white soldiers made it sound as if the People would live exactly as before, only better.

Watching her father solemnly lay down his rifle and his bow and arrows at the feet of the commanding officer, Sarah sensed that life would never be the same.

She had once known a medicine man who had tamed a red-tailed hawk. The bird had been injured and the man fed it and made it well again. He kept the bird tied to a rawhide thong, so it would not escape. Only able to fly short distances, the hawk would never survive in the wild again. But, the medicine man insisted, the bird would not have to worry about enemies, either.

Sarah could see the similarities of the two situations. And yet, she believed the hawk would rather have died in the wild, free and happy, than be bound by a master's rules.

As much as she wished to live peacefully with her white brothers, she did not think her people could live tethered on a leather thong.

Part II

10

Hoofbeats thudded outside Sarah's *karnee*.
She stepped outside into the blazing sun to
see who had ridden up.

"Sarah," called the bearded man on horseback.
"The supplies are here at last. Will you help me
distribute the goods?"

"Yes, Mr. Wasson," Sarah replied. The others
in her tribe called the reservation agent "Long
Beard," but Sarah addressed him by his proper
name. Her relationship with the agent was one
thing that set her apart from her people these
days. Being chosen to help distribute provisions
was another.

It was the summer of 1861. A year had passed
since the war at Pyramid Lake.

Sarah still wore the calico dress, now much-
mended, from her stay at the sisters' school in
California. That was another thing that set her
apart. The dress reminded her of those happier
days at school. Sarah knew she looked different

from the other women, but she did not see herself as an ordinary Numa woman. She *was* different.

Now she sent a brief prayer to the Spirit Father, asking that lengths of dress material be included in the shipment. She wanted very much to make herself a new dress. "Red would be most appreciated," she concluded hopefully.

Mr. Wasson assisted her up on the back of his horse and they rode off across the flat brushland to the agent's house. A large group of People thronged the storehouse.

The men were a ragtag lot, Sarah observed sadly. Some still wore the hickory shirts from the first issue months ago, torn and poorly-mended. Some wore a combination of overalls and buckskins; a few men draped blankets over their nakedness.

As soon as they saw Sarah and the agent riding up, they clamored for his attention.

Sarah slid off the horse, pushing her way through the crowd.

"Be patient," she told the men in her own tongue. In English, she asked Mr. Wasson, "What did we receive this time? Red shirts? Dress goods? Medicine for Pe-sau-you?"

The agent shook his head. "Only flour, Sarah. And not much of that."

"No medicine?" Her friend Pe-sau-you had a terribly sore eye. Mr. Wasson had promised to get medicine for her.

"Not a drop." He led the way into the mostly empty storeroom and shut the door behind him. "I went into Sacramento yesterday and bought medicine myself. I'll send the bill to the government. Though I doubt I'll be reimbursed," he added wryly.

Sarah's glance took in the dusty sacks of flour stacked along one wall. Her expert eye, skilled at measuring allotments, determined there was not enough flour to feed half of the Numa living closest to the agent's house.

"There is not enough flour to give one family an entire sack," she said.

"No," Wasson agreed. "We'll have to divide the flour. Though that will not stretch far, either."

"The Big Father in Washington must think the Indian does not need much to eat," Sarah remarked acidly.

In the last several months, since she had come to live on the Pyramid Lake Reservation, she had seen many promises broken by the white man and was not afraid to speak her mind.

"The Big Father in Washington certainly does not pay attention to the letters I write," the agent said as he began dragging sacks forward. "I might as well be sending smoke signals, for all the answer I receive."

"I know you do your best," Sarah said.

"It's my job, Sarah. I was sent here to manage this reservation." He stopped to wipe sweat from his brow with one of the big red-and-white kerchiefs the Numa prized. It was hot in the storeroom with the door closed. "I had plans to help your people become self-sufficient, so you wouldn't have to depend on government aid," he said.

Sarah refrained from commenting that the People had been self-sufficient long before the coming of the white man. They had never needed government aid before, as long as they had had enough land.

The Pyramid Lake Reservation was sixty miles long and fifteen miles wide. The area encompassed both Pyramid and Muddy lakes. At first the People lived as they always had, in small isolated bands, each headed by a subchief. They fished for *cui-cui*, hunted game, gathered pine nuts and seeds. No white settlers lived on their land. The reservation was theirs alone, according to the treaty between the Numa and the white soldiers. After a few months, the white man's government sent out an agent to oversee the reservation.

When Warren Wasson arrived, he brought with him a bountiful shipment of goods: hickory shirts, overalls, blankets, flannel cloth, fishhooks and line, kettles and tools, flour and meat.

The Numa offered songs of thanks to the Spirit Father the day the supplies were given out. The shirts and overalls were dutifully blessed before being worn; the food blessed before being eaten.

Mr. Wasson, who knew of her speaking skills, asked Sarah to interpret for him. Sarah assisted with the issues, riding from group to group to inform her people that supplies had arrived, and also helped the agent in daily matters involving her people.

He told Sarah of his plans for the reservation. They would have a sawmill and a gristmill, so they could mill their own lumber and grind their own flour. They would raise crops of corn and wheat. They would build a school and send east for a teacher to teach the children to read. This last plan made Sarah's heart catch. More than anything, she wanted to finish her schooling and become a teacher. Her greatest wish was to teach her own people.

But Mr. Wasson's dreams soon turned to ashes. The agent encouraged the People to dig an irrigation ditch. They would need water to run the sawmill and gristmill. Faithfully, day after day, the People bent their backs over shovels in the hot sun. A year and more passed, yet the funds to build the promised mills never came.

Disheartened, the People stopped digging and went back to their isolated bands. Only they did not live as they had before, Sarah noticed. Instead of fishing or hunting to fill their winter stores, the Numa now waited for flour and meat. They did not want to tan deerhide for garments. Putting on white man's shirts, she reflected, was the first step away from life as it had been since ancient times.

Her father complained when he witnessed the skimpy rations of flour doled out later that day.

"This is not how we were meant to exist," he said to Sarah. "Waiting for white man's handouts. What do they care if we starve? We should be free to live as we always have."

"It is worse off the reservation," Sarah said. Mr. Wasson had reported seeing hungry Paiutes camped around the stagecoach stations. They collected manure from the stable floor, sifting the horse droppings for undigested barley.

"Tomorrow we will go see our people along the Humboldt River," her father said.

Over the next few months, Sarah traveled with her father the length and breadth of the reservation, living with the scattered tribes. Since her father was head chief, he felt it was his responsibility to see that each tribe was doing well. Sometimes he rode into white settlements along the borders of the reservation and spoke to gathered crowds. During these dramatic performances, Winnemucca wore his eagle-feathered headdress. Occasionally, two of Winnemucca's men would hold a red-and-white crescent banner over his head, while Sarah interpreted.

She spoke English fluently, as well as Spanish and Shoshone, and her language skills were becoming widely known. She enjoyed working with

Mr. Wasson and representing her tribe in the settlements as her father's interpreter. The white people called her the "Indian princess." As long as her people were not suffering, Sarah was happy.

That summer, the white people in the settlements talked about a big war back East. Warren Wasson told Sarah that Nevada, or Washoe, was now a territory separate from Utah.

"There's talk that it will be made a state soon," he said. "Even before Utah. Because of the silver. President Lincoln needs the income from the silver mines to pay for this war."

Later that year, Wasson left Pyramid Lake. The agency sent a succession of new agents, none of whom lasted long, to manage the reservation. Conditions for the People of Pyramid Lake grew worse very quickly.

None of the new agents cared about the People. They were not interested in helping the Indians become self-sufficient, or even in their day-to-day survival. Sarah worked with corrupt agents, who sold the goods meant for the Indians, either to the People themselves, or to their white friends. One fine issue of farm tools and ready-made clothes like hats, shoes, and shawls were shipped to Salt Lake City, to be sold. Sarah cried as she watched bales of clothing being piled into the wagons, things meant for her people. The People received a few blankets, some blue and red flannel, and two kettles. When some men went around with one leg wrapped in red flannel, all they could do with such skimpy yardage, the white men laughed at them.

During this painful time, Sarah quarreled with her father.

"We must fight for our rights," she told Winnemucca when they heard that their land was gradually being taken over by white squatters. "This land is for our use only. Those men are breaking the treaty."

"White men break promises all the time," her father said. "What can the poor Indian do about it? We cannot make war. The whites would destroy us. We can only pray."

"What good is prayer?" Praying no longer worked for Sarah. Shamans' chants were useless against white men's bullets.

Her father looked at her. "I am proud that my daughter has acquired the ability to talk on paper. But there are things to be learned of life not set down in books."

"There is nothing more important than an education," she countered.

"You should think of marrying," said her father. "It is time you settled down."

She did not want to settle down. Settling down meant a life bent over the cook-fire. "There is no one worth marrying."

Her father pulled thoughtfully on his pipe. "You

know Numa men do not like bold women. They do not make very good wives. Perhaps you should stay with the women from now on. Natchez can talk for me when I go into the white man's camps."

"I will not stay with the women," she said angrily. "I will leave here if what I do does not please you."

True to her word, she left the reservation and lived with some Numa on the outskirts of Virginia City, the best-known mining town in Washoe.

Most of the mining towns that sprang up near the mines were disgraceful settlements of shacks tottering among piles of discarded rock. Virginia City, however, was refined compared to those rough places.

The town prospered from the output of the Comstock Lode, the biggest silver mine in the territory. In the shadow of the Sun Mountain were stately mansions, the luxurious Silver Dollar and Silver Queen hotels, restaurants, schools, stores, churches, saloons galore, and Piper's Opera House.

The Paiutes who camped near Virginia City hung around the Assay Office or Miner's Union Hall, hoping to find work in the mines. Prospectors used the People as slave labor, promising them wages they never intended to pay or paying them with a little flour. The mines were terrible places — timber-roofed tunnels that plunged deep into the bowels of the mountain where the rock was so hot, the miners could only work in brief shifts. The Indian workers were not given many opportunities to rest.

Sarah was shocked when she saw how her people lived. Women rose with the sun and took their baskets to gather scraps of food in the garbage heaps behind the hotels. Children picked up straw, which they gnawed to keep their stomachs from growling.

Using her skill with the needle, Sarah embroidered pillow covers and towels and went from house to house, offering her work for sale. In the "Castle," the finest house in Virginia City, Sarah was allowed to step inside the marble front hall while the maid showed her work to the lady of the house. Sarah marveled at the Comstock-silver doorknobs, the hand-blocked French wallpaper, and the crystal chandeliers from Czechoslovakia. Such opulence was not uncommon in the homes of wealthy miners.

She felt a surge of anger when the haughty maid purchased two pillow slips. Was it fair that the whites had so much while her people were begging scraps from the miners' lunch pails? But she took the money without comment. On her way back through town, Sarah stopped at a store and bought a grammar text.

The storekeeper looked at her curiously. "Can you read?"

"A little. I would like to read better." Sarah

knew the storekeeper was surprised that a "squaw" wanted an education.

Work helped fill her days. Perhaps her father was right. Perhaps she should find a husband.

Kuagunt, a young man, seemed to admire her lively personality. He courted her and Sarah consented to marry him. But the marriage was a mistake.

Although she tried, Sarah found it difficult to be a good Numa wife. She learned too late that her husband was more interested in her livelihood than her lively personality. He made her turn over her earnings so he could buy whiskey. Even though it was illegal to sell liquor to Indians, unscrupulous whites sold it to them anyway.

The worst moment came when her husband threw her grammar book into the fire, instead of looking for kindling. Sarah divorced him for his cruel behavior. In the Numa ceremony, she told him to leave her wickiup forever and the marriage ended.

When she was alone again, she bought another grammar text and often read late into the night by flickering firelight.

One day she heard a commotion in town.

"What is it?" she asked a man.

"President Lincoln made Nevada a state!" he whooped.

Shortly after the statehood of Nevada, the war back East ended. Sarah moved to the town of

Dayton, where she lived with yet another group of Numa. She did not go back to Pyramid Lake. She could not face her father, certain he would not approve of her divorce.

Early one spring morning, a troop of blue-coated soldiers rode into camp. Sarah interpreted for the captain.

"Your people have been stealing cattle from the settlers at Harney Lake," Captain Wells accused. "We will not tolerate such behavior. We will kill anyone that gets in our way."

The captain galloped away. Sarah's heart flew into her throat. They were heading in the direction of the reservation! There was no time to warn her people. The captain's brigade rode swiftly, charged with anger.

She waited all day, knotted with anxiety. What was happening to her people?

Late that night, a horse skidded into camp. Sarah's sister Elma jumped off the pony and burst into tears. Her hair and clothes were in wild disarray. She could barely speak, but Sarah pieced together her story.

Blue-coats raided the camp by Muddy Lake, shooting women as they tended their cook-fires, shooting old men who were placidly fishing on the shore, shooting children before they could run to their mothers. Everyone was dead, Elma told Sarah, except their father and some men who were hunting at Stillwater. Their mother and

Mary were at Pyramid Lake, so they were safe.

"How did you get away?" Sarah asked.

"I jumped on our father's best horse and rode like the devil," Elma replied. "The blue-coats were busy setting our camp on fire." She drew a shuddering breath. "There is more. The babies . . . after everyone had been killed, they took the babies in their cradleboards and *threw* them into the fire! Oh, Sarah, they burned our baby brother alive!"

Sarah held her sister. Such a terrible thing for her sister — for anyone — to witness.

"How could the whites be such barbarians?" Elma sobbed.

"I do not know," Sarah said, clenching her fists. Only heartless monsters tossed babies into fire. And yet they spoke so highly of their religion and talked to their God three times a day. What would those men say to their God after what they had done?

"Grandfather was wrong," Sarah said. "He believed the whites were his brothers. They are not my brothers!"

She had tried to live by her grandfather's wishes and get along with the whites. But she could not do so any longer.

11

Sarah rubbed the grimy shirt over the washboard, skinning her knuckles as she tried to scrub out the worst of the dirt. Fortunately, Mr. Nugent was not particular about his laundry. He did not care much about his appearance, seldom changing his shirt or shaving.

The slovenly agent didn't care much about the Indians he was supposed to be helping, either. When Sarah returned to the reservation in 1866, at Natchez's urging, she was appalled to find her people barely scraping by. Most were poorly dressed, many were sick, all were hungry.

"*Where* are the provisions going?" Sarah asked her brother.

"Mr. Nugent sells our goods to his white friends. We receive nothing." A muscle in his jaw tightened. "Everywhere the citizens say the red devils are killing their cattle. You know it is not true, Sarah. The white settlers tell these things to the army to make war on us. The soldiers come to protect them and buy their beef and grain. The settlers get fat by this."

The reality of the situation made Sarah furious. Even if her people were starving, they would not dishonor the tribe by killing livestock that did not belong to them. The Numa who still upheld the treaty stayed obediently on the reservation and went hungry. Those who no longer trusted the whites fought back. Troops were being marshaled daily to "take care" of the suddenly warlike Numa. And then there were those who simply left, dispirited and broken.

Sarah's father was one of the latter. After his baby son had been murdered at Muddy Lake, Chief Winnemucca retreated north to live with a distant tribe in the Oregon territory. He sent word to Natchez that he would never return to his homeland. Shortly after Winnemucca left, Sarah's mother died — from grief, Sarah fervently believed. Her older sister Mary fell ill and died, too. Elma was also changed by the killings at Muddy Lake. She married a white man and went to live on his ranch in Montana.

During that long autumn, Sarah had never felt so alone. Her life was like a seed basket that had come unraveled and she did not know how to stitch the frazzled plaits together.

When Natchez found her living again in Virginia City, he asked her to come back to the reservation to stay with him and his wife. Sarah agreed. Perhaps her brother and her old friends could help her reweave the frayed pieces of her life.

But when she saw the faces of children pinched with hunger, the hopeless expressions in the eyes of her girlhood friends, Sarah knew they could not help her. If anything, she would have to help *them*.

Her first act was to go to the agent's house and demand work. Mr. Nugent, narrowing his pale eyes at this bold Indian woman, thrust an enormous bundle of dirty laundry at her.

"You can wash my clothes," he drawled.

"For how much payment?" Sarah asked staunchly.

"We'll see." The agent slammed the door in her face.

Sarah went back to camp to fetch her sister-in-law. The two women set up washtubs and heated water. They worked most of the day, scrubbing sheets and shirts and overalls. When the clothes had dried in the hot sun and they had folded the laundry, Sarah knocked on the agent's door again. Mr. Nugent opened the door.

"How much pay?" Sarah indicated the pile of clean clothes.

Grunting his disapproval that Indians should be paid anything, Mr. Nugent gave Sarah a small sack of flour.

Sarah survived that winter by washing the agent's clothes in return for flour. The rest of the time her family had only seeds, which Sarah made into mush. Her own face became thin.

Spring arrived and the white farmers began plowing fields. *We must learn to do this*, Sarah resolved. If her people sold grain, they could live on the limited land of their reservation. There was not enough land to support them in the old way of hunting and fishing. The People would have to change in order to survive. But they needed help to do this.

"Show us how to plant crops," she asked the agent. "Give us wagons and plows and harnesses."

Nugent rudely spat a wad of tobacco at her feet. Disgusted, she went back to her camp. Of all the agents the Big Father in Washington had sent to Pyramid Lake, Nugent was the worst. He showed his lack of morals a few weeks later when he sold gunpowder to an Indian. It was against the law for the People to buy ammunition, but Nugent cared only for money.

As soon as the Indian crossed the river, he was shot by one of Nugent's men for possession of gunpowder. Word of the man's death reached the camp and the People went wild. *This* time the agent would die.

Natchez turned to Sarah. "What shall we do?" As peace chief, he did not believe in revenge, yet how much more bloodshed could their people endure? No good would come of murdering the agent. The blame would fall on them all.

Sarah struggled with her own conscience. Nugent was not worth the air he breathed. Her grandfather had lived for the return of his white brothers, and had died with one wish on his lips — that they all try to get along. She didn't wish the agent to be killed — she didn't wish anyone dead — but she could not help that man.

Natchez saddled his horse and rushed to warn the agent. When he returned, he told Sarah that Nugent refused to heed his warning. "He said he would show the red devils how to fight," he concluded angrily.

"Then there is nothing for us to do," Sarah said.

"No." Her brother shook his head. "If we do nothing, we will all die at the hands of the angry whites who will avenge Nugent's death."

In council, Natchez ordered ten of his warriors to watch the river crossing and waylay any of their people bent on revenge.

"Kill them if necessary," Natchez said grimly. "It is better that we kill some of our own people than *all* be killed."

Sarah felt sickened by her brother's order. But she knew he was right. Better a few should die than the entire tribe. She waited with her brother that night, afraid to sleep. The next morning one of the scouts ran to their lodge.

Natchez hurried to meet him. "Did Nugent go away?"

"Yes, but one of Nugent's men is dead and another is almost dead," the scout panted. "Our people also stole many horses."

At this serious news, Natchez took more men to track down the renegades. Later that day Sarah received a letter, carried by another of Natchez's scouts.

"Who gave you this?" she asked, taking the paper in astonishment. She had never received a letter in her life.

"The officer at the soldier's hiding place." The "hiding place" was Fort Churchill, on the Carson River.

People pressed in closely as Sarah unfolded the paper. She frowned at the officer's handwriting. After reading it four times, she was able to decipher the writing.

"The letter is from a Captain Jerome. I do not know who he is. He wants me and my brother to meet him here tonight."

"Your brother is not here," her uncle Wa-he said. "Can you answer this Jerome on paper?"

Sarah shook her head. "I have nothing to write with. I have no ink. Nor pen."

"You and your brother are the only means of saving us," Wa-he insisted. "Take a stick to write with — take anything."

Sarah knew Wa-he and the others doubted her ability to talk on paper. More importantly, the lives of everyone on the reservation were at stake. If she and Natchez failed to meet the captain, he might believe they were involved in the killings. She *had* to answer his letter.

"Make me a stick with a sharp point," she said. "And bring me some fish's blood." On the back of Captain Jerome's letter, she carefully composed her reply, using the pointed stick for a pen and fish blood for ink.

Hon. Sir, she wrote, *My brother is not here. I am looking for him every minute. We will go as soon as he comes in. Yours, S.W.*

Sending the letter to Fort Churchill with the same scout, Sarah waited for Natchez. When he arrived a short time later, she told him about the meeting. Natchez ate, changed horses, and they rode to Fort Churchill as fast as their ponies could carry them. Sarah told Captain Jerome what she knew of the situation. The captain asked her how much her people had to eat.

"At the present, nothing," she replied. "We are hoping the fish will run upriver soon so we can catch them."

The captain thought a moment. "Your agent is not an honest man. He tried to sell me beef intended for your people. Sarah, go back to your people and tell them not to be afraid of us. I will go to my commanding officer and see what can be done about getting your people food."

Within two days, the army sent three wagons

of provisions to the reservation. Captain Jerome met once more with Sarah.

"I have a letter from my commander. He wants to know if your father is here with you."

Sarah began to cry. "My father has not been here since the soldiers killed my baby brother. He has gone to live in the mountains. He says he will die there."

Captain Jerome's voice was kind. "Don't cry, Sarah. You and your brother will go with me to bring your father back. It's not safe for an old man to be out there, without protection."

"I do not know if he will come."

"If he comes in, he'll be cared for by the army," Captain Jerome told her. "All of your people will be fed by the army post at Fort McDermitt."

"What do you think about it?" Natchez asked his sister.

Sarah was afraid for her father. She knew what liars the white people were, but Captain Jerome *had* sent them food. Going with the soldiers meant they would have to leave Pyramid Lake, but at least they would not starve.

"I think we should go get our father if we can," she said. She turned to Captain Jerome. "We will go with you."

It took them twenty-eight days to reach Fort McDermitt, near the Oregon border, in high summer heat. Sarah was exhausted by the time they reached the fort. Long stone buildings faced distant mountains. Major Dudley Seward gave Sarah her own room in the headquarters. When they had rested and eaten, they met Colonel McElroy who expressed his concerns about their father.

"He's too old to be out in this bad country. The settlers have sent for General Crook to kill all the Indians who are not on reservations. I'm afraid for your father out there. I will be his friend and fight for him."

Even though McElroy's remarks had been directed to her brother, Sarah spoke up. "Colonel, my good father has never done anything unkind to the white people. The soldiers killed my baby brother at Muddy Lake. This is what drove my father away. We have not seen him for two years."

Natchez said, "It is too bad the way the white people always say that Indians have black hearts. If you will give me your heart and hand, I will try to get my father to come to you."

"I'll send one company of cavalry with you," McElroy promised. "Your sister can stay here and interpret for the Indians already here. I have about twenty-five Queen's River Indians in my care. I will pay your sister sixty-five dollars a month."

"I do not want any soldiers to go with me," Natchez said. "My people will think I have brought the soldiers to kill them. Give me a paper to tell the white people who I am, so *they* will not kill *me*. You know, colonel, the white men like to kill us Indians."

Sarah was proud of her brother. The way he spoke up to the commander showed that the People had a sense of humor. But she was afraid to be left alone in the camp, even though Natchez had asked that no soldiers talk to his sister. After Natchez left, Sarah went to McElroy and told him her fears.

"I want you to give orders to your soldiers not to go to our people's camp at any time, and also issue the same order to the citizens," she said.

McElroy complied, and the People lived peacefully in their own camp next to the fort.

Sarah wanted to stay with the Queen's River girls in the camp, but her position as interpreter made her different. Her schooling gave her power — she could talk on paper and make commanding officers issue orders. She had grown up a great deal since she had last seen her father.

When the horses appeared on the horizon one morning, everyone ran out of their tents, throwing their robes on the ground to welcome the newcomers.

Natchez's mission had been successful. He had persuaded Chief Winnemucca and four hundred and ninety People to come to Camp McDermitt. Sarah stood at the front of the welcoming throng, waiting to greet her father. Would he still be angry with her? Would he remember their last quarrel?

Chief Winnemucca slid off his mount and embraced her. "My daughter," he said, crying, and Sarah knew it was all right between them again.

12

The faint light of dawn woke Sarah. She rose and put on her snug-fitting black dress with the green fringe, then went down to the stream to wash. After eating a hasty meal of cold beans, she hurried to the store in the army compound.

Numa women were already lined up at the door, baskets over their arms. Sarah unlocked the door and began issuing the day's supplies. As she looked past the headquarters building to the village of tents beyond, she thought how much had changed since her people came to Fort McDermitt.

Life in an army camp was very different from life on a reservation. Sarah adjusted quickly to the soldiers' way of doing things. Food and supplies were not doled out haphazardly as they had been on the reservation. The People did not have to rely on the fairness of an agent to survive. The army took care of them in an organized manner.

Every morning at five o'clock, Sarah gave out

daily rations. And such generous rations! A pound and a half of meat for every grown person and a loaf of bread. The soldier-cooks actually baked wonderful bread every day for the Indians.

The women shuffled forward, each with a numbered tag fastened to a leather thong around her neck. The first woman in line said, "Number eighty-one. Five people in my family."

Sarah put four and a half pounds of dried beef and three loaves of bread into her basket. Then she recorded the amount in a notebook. Every morsel had to be accounted for — that was the way things were done in soldiers' camps.

The line seemed to stretch for miles. It took Sarah a long time to give out the daily supplies. Her back hurt, but at least everyone had enough and she did not have to turn anyone away hungry. Filling her own basket last, she locked the supply door and headed back to her tent.

She was tired. She didn't mind the work, but she missed the freedom of the old life. Here they were well-fed, but the regimen of army life meant there was little time for herself.

Her father was sitting cross-legged outside their tent, replacing the worn feathers on his arrows. He was dressed in the dark blue uniform coat and trousers all men wore.

The soldiers gave the men uniforms, but the women and children had only blankets. The government did not supply its army with any clothing other than uniforms. Sarah had bought the green-trimmed black dress with her earnings as Colonel McElroy's interpreter. She wished the other women had money for material.

"Good morning, Father," Sarah greeted, setting the heavy basket on the ground. "How are you this day?"

Winnemucca grunted, an indication he was not in a fine mood. "I see you have brought our daily meat and bread."

"Yes. In three days time, we will have beans and coffee and rice." At the beginning of each month, Sarah issued additional supplies of coffee, beans, rice, sugar, salt, and pepper.

Her father worked on his arrows for a while. Then he said, "I do not like living entirely on the goodness of the soldiers. It is not right for us to be handed our meat and rice. It is not our way."

"But the soldiers want to take care of us," Sarah said. "It is better than starving on the reservation. We were like prisoners there." She pushed away the image of women wearing tags on leather thongs, like the hawk that had been captured. In a way, they were prisoners here as well, but at least they had food.

"It is wrong," her father insisted. "See what happens when we are not working for ourselves." With his arrow, he pointed to a group of men playing a gambling game.

Lee Winnemucca was laughing at a mistake the

other team had just made. Sarah's younger brother was tall and smooth-skinned. Sarah noted that Lee's team was doing very well, judging from the high scores of stones on their side.

"Our men often play gambling games," she said.

"Yes, but not the day long. It is fine to play gambling games when the hunting is done. Our people are too idle. It is not right," her father repeated.

Sarah had to agree with her father on one point. Without work, the men were becoming bored. And boredom, she knew, often led to foolish quarrels.

That night Chief Winnemucca held a council. He told his people they should not expect the soldiers to feed and clothe them until they died. They were perfectly able to support themselves and should not idle their days away in child's play.

The chief's voice rang with authority. "I want the men to go on hunting expeditions and bring in rabbit and venison and other game. I want the women to gather grass-seed and dig roots for the coming winter. We cannot depend on the soldiers. Their food supplies are not ever-bearing, like the juniper tree."

Then her father spoke to her. "Sarah, you will go tell the colonel what I have said. Tell him my men need ammunition to go hunting."

"We cannot just ask for the soldiers' ammunition," she said. "We must pay for it."

He father considered. "Tell the colonel to give us the ammunition and to make a record of it and bring it to me. I will see that the powder is paid for."

"We do not need powder for hunting," she argued. "If the women are careful with their rations, they could save and sell some of it and buy calico and necessary things for their children."

"That is how we will pay for the ammunition," her father stated. "You will go tell the colonel what I have said."

Sarah did not say anymore, for she was too angry with her father to speak. He didn't see that the women and children were poorly clothed. Why couldn't he sacrifice his pride and help the women? The men thought of hunting while their children ran about in rags.

The colonel agreed to her father's request, but something else was on his mind.

Four hundred of the People were living at Camp C.F. Smith, some sixty-five miles away. The Paiutes were trying to take care of themselves, but in that arid region game was scarce and the army post was not big enough to support so many.

"We need to bring them here," the colonel said. "We can feed them all. How many companies do you think it will take to escort them here?"

"None," Sarah said. "You and I could escort them. Or my brother Lee and I."

Colonel McElroy was astonished. "Only you and

125

your young brother? Sarah, that is a lot of people to relocate. You are just a girl."

"I am the daughter of a chief," she reminded him quietly. "I know my people, colonel. They will come if I talk to them."

In the end, Colonel McElroy agreed to let Sarah go with him and one other man. At Camp C.F. Smith, Sarah went into council with the People, convincing them to move to the bigger army post. She talked all night, describing the conditions at Fort McDermitt and patiently answering many questions. In the morning, the People were ready to leave.

Colonel McElroy shook his head in disbelief. "I don't know how you did it, Sarah."

"It was not so difficult," she told him. "We try to rule our people by explaining things to them. When they understand, there is no trouble."

The journey took two days. Sarah requested horses for the men and fifteen wagons to transport the women and children. She rode at the head of the caravan, glad to prove to the colonel that the People could behave in an orderly manner.

Now nine hundred Indians lived in the camp next to Fort McDermitt. Sarah rose before dawn to issue daily rations. The line of women with baskets and numbered tags snaked across the compound. Sarah was glad to serve her people, even though the job was exhausting.

One morning a young lieutenant was waiting

for her when she locked the store. His name was Edward Bartlett.

"Let me carry that," Lieutenant Bartlett offered, taking her basket. "May I walk you back to camp, Sarah?"

Sarah knew she should not speak to the man without her brothers or father present. Yet she talked to Colonel McElroy all the time, either interpreting or about other business. What was the harm in letting this nice young man carry her basket?

They chatted as they strolled outside the fort. When Edward took her arm gently above the elbow to steer her around a campfire, she felt a thrill ripple up her backbone. She felt as fragile as one of the china figures in Margaret Ormsby's parlor.

At her tent, he said, "I'll see you tomorrow."

Sarah's father was watching from the shade of the tent. "*Ha-ja-ou-sow?*" he asked.

"His name is Lieutenant Bartlett," Sarah obstinately answered in English. She knew her father disapproved of her walking out with a white man, but she liked Edward Bartlett and would not be cowed by her father. Not this time.

"What are Lieutenant Bartlett's intentions?" her father asked.

"Father, I have only walked out with the man once. How should I know what his intentions are?"

"I will ask your brothers about this Lieutenant

Bartlett," Winnemucca said, closing his eyes to end the discussion.

Both Lee and Natchez knew Edward Bartlett. By the time they talked to Sarah about him, she was in love with the young officer and had decided to marry him.

"Bartlett drinks," Natchez warned. "He walks crooked most nights. He would not be a good husband."

"That is what you say," Sarah countered. "I know Edward is a good, kind man. I am going to marry him."

Her father broke in. "It is forbidden by white man's law for our people to marry whites."

Only in the state of Nevada, Sarah knew. But marriage was possible in Utah Territory. At the beginning of 1871, Sarah and Edward eloped to Salt Lake City, where they were married. After a short honeymoon, they returned to Fort McDermitt, where Sarah set up housekeeping in the married officers' quarters.

When she went to see her father, he barely spoke to her.

"I hope you are happy," he said curtly.

"I am," she told him. "Edward is a wonderful husband." This was not quite the truth. Since their return, Edward spent more time in the saloon than with his new bride. And the white officers' wives resented Sarah's presence in their quarters.

Her father eyed her new dress, the latest fashion. Sarah wore her long hair loose, with the sides pulled back with tortoiseshell combs and a fringe of bangs on her forehead.

"You dress like a white woman," he said. "You speak like a white person. You are married to a white man. But you are still one of the People. You cannot change who you are."

Sarah was irritated, mostly because her father had been right about Edward all along. "It is you who must change, Father. It will do no good for us to cling to the old ways. All of our people must learn to change."

Change came sooner than even Sarah expected. The Big Father in Washington, President Grant, decreed that Indians were wards of the government and must live on reservations. This meant the People would have to leave Fort McDermitt.

Sarah went to Colonel McElroy. "What can be done? We do not want to leave here."

"The Bureau of Indian Affairs claims the army is spoiling the Indians." He shook his head. "I have written letters about how we have found the Indians starving, but no one listens."

Sarah decided someone would listen to *her*. That night she wrote a letter to Major Henry Douglas, who had come to Fort McDermitt to talk to the People about moving to reservations. She explained the hardships her people had suffered at Pyramid Lake Reservation. The major passed her letter on to the Commissioner of Indian Affairs. But she heard no reply.

She wrote again. And again. Sarah persistently wrote to the commission.

"Talking on paper does no good," Natchez scoffed.

"It is the only way to win this war," Sarah said. "We cannot win against the white man with prayers. We have to use *their* weapons — words. I will go to San Francisco and talk to the commissioner personally."

Wearing her new dress, Sarah set off for San Francisco, this time by train. Indians were allowed to ride the freight cars free. In San Francisco, she spoke to officials who listened to her eloquent pleas but offered no solution. Her cause gathered publicity, though, and she read about herself, "the fiery Indian princess," in the newspapers.

Back at Fort McDermitt, Sarah sadly admitted her failure.

"Words did not work?" Natchez asked.

She sighed. "Not this time."

Discouraged, she turned her attention to matters close to home. Her marriage to Edward Bartlett was a mistake. With her earnings from her interpreting job, she obtained a legal divorce. No longer married, she moved back into her father's tent.

Winnemucca was not pleased. "How many times are you to be married and divorced, daughter?"

Sarah did not answer. In her father's eyes, she was disgraced for marrying Edward Bartlett in the first place.

"We are leaving," Winnemucca told her. "Our people will not go to the reservation where there is no game and they are prey to white man's sicknesses. Will you come with us?"

"Where will you go?"

"To the north, where we can still live free."

"There is *no place* where we are free. It is best to stay here on the army post, Father. Let the soldiers throw us out if they have to."

But the chief had made up his mind. He took the People who wanted to go with him and left Fort McDermitt.

Sarah watched them leave, fighting tears. She knew she could not live on the army base indefinitely. When the white people made a law, they took action. But she could not aimlessly wander around the countryside either. Sooner or later, there would be a confrontation with the whites.

More importantly, Sarah could not go back to a life of roasting seeds and weaving baskets. She had some schooling, and had seen the world beyond the borders of her homeland. She felt divided. Half of her wanted her people to be happy and free; the other half desired the best of the white man's world.

As the last pony disappeared down the trail, Sarah felt a heaviness around her heart. Her marriage had failed. Her mission to San Francisco had failed. Her family was gone once again.

And she herself had no place to go.

13

"You cannot refuse," Lee said to his sister. "The People need you."

Sarah folded the letter her brother had just brought her with a final motion. "I do not want to go interpret for Mr. Parrish on his reservation. What do I know of this man?"

"He is the new agent for Malheur Reservation," Lee told her. "The last agent was not a good man. But I think Mr. Sam Parrish will be different."

Sarah turned to the man who had been listening quietly. "What should I do, Father? Would you go with me if I should accept the job?"

It was spring, 1875. After months of rootless wandering, Sarah had come to see her father in Camp Harney, Oregon. She had lived with various groups of her people, always near towns. She made a scant living peddling her needlework, but was not happy. The land was not the land she knew. The northern country made her feel homesick.

The army camp on Lake Harney was not supposed to be taking care of Indians, but the officers in this post did not strictly obey the Bureau of Indian Affairs. Sarah longed to settle down somewhere, but she was reluctant to go to a reservation. Memories of those days at Pyramid Lake burned deep.

When Lee rode in from Malheur with the letter from the agent, Sarah wondered if this was another attempt to trick "outside" Indians into moving to a reservation.

She was surprised to hear her father reply, "Yes, I will go with you to Malheur."

That settled her mind. If her father was willing to live on a reservation again, then she would give it another chance.

They left early the next morning so they could cover the fifty miles in one day. When they arrived, Sam Parrish welcomed them heartily. Parrish gave her a small room, offering wages of forty dollars a month. Her room and board would only cost her fifteen dollars a month.

"The previous interpreter has bad eyes," Mr. Parrish told her. "Your brother Natchez took him to San Francisco to see a doctor. I need someone to talk for me."

Sarah nodded. "That would be my cousin Jarry. Many of our people have sore eyes. The campfire smoke is bad for us. I have no place else to go, Mr. Parrish. I accept your offer."

The reservation was in poor shape. The agent before Mr. Parrish had cheated the People by selling them supplies at outrageous prices. Jarry reported the agent to the officers of Camp Harney. The old agent was discharged and Sam Parrish took over.

He called Winnemucca and the other men to his office for a meeting. "This reservation is yours. I will teach you how to work so you can do for yourselves by-and-by. I will build a schoolhouse and my brother's wife will teach your children how to read like the white children. I want to teach you all to do like the white people. The white man gets some land and works it as best he can. You will do that, too."

After Sarah translated this speech, her father asked his people, "What do you think of what the new agent says?"

Natchez spoke first. "The white men believe that their way of life is best. They work their land until it is worn out, then they move on to work another piece of land. They do not try to get along with what they have. They always want more."

Winnemucca grunted in agreement. "My son speaks the truth. The white man labors all day, but he seems to take no pleasure from the land that serves him."

Sarah broke in. "Mr. Parrish is not talking to us about whether the white man's life or the In-

135

dian's life is better. I think he is trying to help us the only way he knows."

Winnemucca spoke to Parrish. "My son Natchez says if we do not do as we are told, we will not get along at all. My children" — he indicated Sarah and her brother — "talk for you and tell us what you say. We will work at whatever we must."

Not everyone was willing to obey the agent. The Harney Lake chief, who was half-Numa, half-Bannock, grumbled his protest.

"I am not going to work," Oytes announced. "My men and I have our own work to do. We must hunt for our children."

"All right, Oytes," Parrish said. "You can do as you like."

One of Oytes' men spoke up. "We want to work with you. Let this man go."

Oytes went his own way. Sarah told the agent the People would be happier if they could also hunt and fish.

Parrish nodded, then explained each person's duties. Three men were chosen to become black-smiths; three more to be carpenters. One group planted potatoes, turnips, and watermelons. Others cut rails for fences. Most of the men began digging an irrigation ditch. After a week, Parrish called Sarah into his office.

"I am glad your people are working so hard," he told her. "But I don't like to see the old men and women out there. The men are too old and the women can prepare their husbands' meals."

Sarah related the agent's concerns. The women went back to tending to family matters, but the old men did not mind working and continued to dig alongside the younger men.

The ten-foot wide ditch grew every day. Sarah remembered the slow, laborious effort to dig an irrigation ditch at Pyramid Lake. It was never finished. But the ditch at Malheur was already two and a half miles long in six short weeks. The schoolhouse was built with equal speed. Sarah could not wait — Mr. Parrish had said she could teach!

The summer passed quickly. Soon it was time to harvest their crops. Mr. Parrish called another meeting.

"Sarah," he said, "tell your people they have worked with good cheer. The other agent told me you were lazy."

When Sarah translated, her father laughed, "What can Parrish expect to hear from a man who was lazy himself?"

Parrish smiled. "I will do all I can while I am with you. After you have cut your hay, you can go hunting."

Eager to hunt again, the men cut the hay quickly. Mr. Parrish gave each man powder, lead, and caps.

The men returned laden with game and venison.

Chief Winnemucca did not come back to Malheur, but went south to Pyramid Lake to see how his people were getting along there. Oytes seemed to think he was head chief in Winnemucca's absence. He hung around Winnemucca's men and made remarks. He claimed he had special powers, that bullets could not kill him and that he could make the People sick if he wanted. Sarah knew Oytes was angry because he had not been given powder for the hunt.

"I am afraid of that man," she confided to Egan, chief of the Snake River Numa.

"Don't mind him," Egan reassured her. "He is nobody."

A few days later, a group of Columbia River Indians came to trade with the People. Although the People had traded with the Columbia River tribe in the past, Sarah's father had warned them not to let the troublemakers on the reservation.

Oytes welcomed the Columbia River warriors after they gave him three horses and encouraged the People to trade their furs for horses. Sarah reported this to Sam Parrish, but before Parrish could take action, Oytes took thirty men off the reservation.

Oytes swaggered back three weeks later. "I want you to talk to your Parrish," he said to Sarah. "Tell him my men and I are going to live with our brothers on the Columbia River. I cannot call that white man my brother."

When Oytes left, Parrish said to Sarah, "Tomorrow is ration day. Will you help me distribute the goods?"

In addition to the usual meat and flour, there were ten yards of calico for every woman, flannel for underwear, pantaloon fabric, handkerchiefs, shoes, stockings, shawls, red blankets, and, as a special treat, looking glasses. Sarah declined anything for herself. She was earning her own money.

Winter passed. Sarah bought a stove to heat her room. She loved being independent. In May the schoolhouse was finished. Mrs. Parrish, the wife of the agent's brother, was the teacher. Sarah was her assistant. She gave up interpreting to teach the children English. Her cousin Jarry, nearly blind, resumed his old job as interpreter.

On the first day of May, the school officially opened with Mrs. Parrish at the organ, playing a rousing hymn. Students packed the building, and women thronged the schoolyard to hear the music. Everyone sang, even those who could not speak a word of English. Sarah had never been so happy.

At the end of the first day, Sarah and Mrs. Parrish took attendance.

"Three hundred and five boys, twenty-three young men, sixty-nine girls, and nineteen young women!" Mrs. Parrish pretended to swoon. "What a lot of students!"

Sarah laughed. She loved this woman who was so kind to the little children. Her greatest dream had come true — she was teaching her people.

The reservation was running smoothly. The People were building a road and had planted acres of crops. Three weeks after the school had opened, Sam Parrish held a special meeting in the schoolhouse. Sarah already knew the sad news.

"I have received a letter from our Big Father in Washington. I have to leave here. Another agent will take my place."

Winnemucca stood. "You shall not leave me and my people."

"It is not for me to say," Parrish replied regretfully.

Sarah's father followed the agent back to his house. "I do not want anyone but you. I am going to see the soldiers. They will keep you here for me."

"They can do nothing against the government."

Sarah's father was silent.

Parrish said, "Come with me, Winnemucca. I want to give you some things."

"I do not want anything," the chief said. The People never clung to possessions belonging to their closest friends.

Sarah whispered to her father, "You had better take what he gives you. The white people give each other things to remember each other by." Her father accepted the shirts and shoes. But when Parrish left, her father left the very next day.

The new agent arrived. His name was Reinhart. He had a hard face and manner. The People worked in the fields the first week and showed up at the agent's house Saturday evening to collect their week's wages. Reinhart opened a record book and began writing: *Blankets, six dollars; shoes, three dollars, coffee, two and a half pounds for a dollar —*

"What are you doing?" Sarah asked him.

"The rations you people have had must be paid for," Reinhart said. "You will work to pay for those things."

Many of the men left, disgusted. Egan said, "Sam Parrish sent for those things and you want us to pay for them?"

"If you don't like my way of doing things, you can all leave," Reinhart retorted.

Outside, the agent grabbed a little boy by the ear and kicked him. "He laughed at me," Reinhart told Sarah. "No one laughs at me. Not even a white man."

Sarah was so angry, she walked away before she hit the man herself.

That night the People came to her, afraid they would starve that winter.

"We will wait and see what he will do," Sarah advised. "If he does not do right by us, I will tell the soldiers at Camp Harney."

Jarry took Sarah aside. "I do not think it is up to you to tell the soldiers."

"I will go if it is necessary!" she said. She had seen her cousin in deep conversation with Reinhart and was wary. Now she had two men to watch: Reinhart and her cousin.

The situation did not improve. Reinhart was stingy with rations and he refused to pay the People for their work. Egan demanded to see the agent.

"I want you to tell everything I say to this man," Egan said to Sarah. She nodded. As Egan spoke, she translated.

"Did the government send you here to drive us off our land?" the chief asked. "Did the Big Father say, go and kill off all the Indians, so you can have our land for yourselves? Do you see that high mountain over there? There is nothing but rocks there. Is that where the Big Father wants us to go? I know the white man will come and say, 'Go away, Indians. I want those rocks to make me a beautiful home!' "

Reinhart started to protest.

Egan was not finished. "Tomorrow I am going to tell the soldiers what you are doing."

"Go live with the soldiers, for all I care," was Reinhart's response.

Sarah thought Egan had spoken well. All he had said was true. Reinhart did not care about them — he only wanted money. For months her people had waited to see if the agent would change, but it was clear he would not. Now it was time to take action.

The next morning, she saddled her horse and rode to Camp Harney to report the conditions at Malheur. The commanding officer listened, then told her to write a report and send it to Washington. Sarah spent an entire night writing her report. After the chiefs signed it, she sent it to Washington.

Reinhart stormed into her room a few days later. "I heard from the officer at Camp Harney you spoke to. You're fired!"

Sarah stayed another three weeks, trying to figure out where she would go. Once Reinhart threatened to shoot and kill a little boy because the child had said something he didn't like. Sarah could no longer defend her people against that man.

She left the reservation and was once more homeless.

14

The dishes and pans were finished. Sarah draped the towel on its nail by the washtub, then picked up the basin and carried it outside to empty. Flinging the water on the flower bed Mrs. Courly was trying to grow in this harsh land, she glanced up at the Strawberry Mountains that horseshoed the valley. The evening star hung between the peaks, like a solitary diamond.

Sarah knew about such things as diamonds. Mrs. Courly wore one in a finger-ring. On her trips to San Francisco, Sarah had glimpsed the luxuries the white people coveted — fur coats and gold-headed walking sticks. Whites were not content having enough food and a warm blanket. They always wanted more — more land, more cattle, more money.

The sight of the solitary star made Sarah feel sad. It was 1878. She had been away from her people for two years. Reinhart would not allow her to set foot on Malheur Reservation. She had a good job keeping house for Mrs. Courly. Sarah had been able to buy her own wagon and a team of horses. As long as she had her independence, she could endure the loneliness.

Or so she believed.

She missed her father and her brothers. She did not even know where her father was at the moment. For a time he and Lee lived at Pyramid Lake. But now Natchez and Lee were back at Malheur. And there was Elma, who was far away in Montana. Sarah never dreamed her family would be so scattered. And that she would be all alone.

She remembered the time she went with the People to charm the antelope. They had never been so free, so much a part of their homeland. That time was gone forever.

She picked up the basin and turned to go back inside when she saw them — Natchez and Lee, tethering their ponies to the big tree in the dooryard. Had she conjured them up, since she had been thinking about them?

"Yes, it is your brothers," Natchez said. "We have come to see you, Sarah. What a hard time we had getting over those mountains! And we have been a long time without food."

"Come inside and have something to eat," she said.

Mrs. Courly bustled about, fixing meat and bread for the visitors. Then she left the room so Sarah could speak to her brothers in private.

Lee took a second helping of meat. "This puts me in mind of old times, when meat and bread were plenty."

"Why have you come?" Sarah asked bluntly. She was glad to see her brothers, but they clearly wanted something from her.

"We know that you are always ready to help your people," Natchez said. "The agent Reinhart will not give us anything to eat. Our children are crying for food. There is nothing to be gathered this time of year. Will you go with us to Camp Harney and talk to the officers there, or go to Washington for us?"

Washington! Sarah's jaw dropped. They wanted her to go all the way to Washington to talk to the Big Father!

"I have no money to go to Washington," she replied, as if she would ever dare to make such a journey. "And you know that Reinhart banished me from the reservation for talking to the officers at Camp Harney. There is nothing I can do."

Dejected, her brothers left. Sarah watched them from the window. She knew terrible things were happening to her people. Everywhere there was unrest between the Indians and the whites. Her people, and other Indians, were dying of diseases the white men brought and starving because the white men took more land every day to farm or graze cattle.

But Sarah felt like the solitary star in the sky. What could one person do to help?

A month later, her brothers returned.

"You are still here!" Natchez cried with relief. "We were afraid you had gone away. Reinhart drove us out of Malheur. We are trying to live on the river by catching salmon, but it is very hard."

Then he told Sarah about the Bannocks, a tribe from Idaho, who were living on the river also. A couple of Bannocks had shot two white men for abusing their women and the band came to the reservation, thinking the agent would let them stay. But when they saw the grim situation at Malheur, the Bannocks chose to live along the river.

Once more Natchez pleaded with Sarah to help them. Once again, she declined. She had her wagon and her team and her routine with Mrs. Courly. She did not want to leave.

"You are hiding here like a coyote licking his wounds," her brother accused as he mounted up.

Was she hiding? Sarah had needed a quiet place to live and time to heal. She had worked very hard for both the whites and her people and she had been deeply hurt. Perhaps the time for healing was over. Although she didn't trust the whites, she could no longer ignore the call to help her people. But she didn't know how to help them.

Natchez came again. "The Bannocks are planning a great war," he reported. "They are hungry and tired of empty promises from the whites. They are saying all the tribes should rise up against the whites and kill them. Even the dead will rise again and join the fight. Our father refuses to join them."

Sarah shuddered at the thought of an all-out war against the whites. So many people would die and her people could never win.

"Have you come to tell me this?" she asked.

"Our people are begging you to go to Washington for them."

Sarah threw up her hands. "Why do you come to me? If it was in my power I would be happy to help you, but I am powerless. I am just a woman. You have your interpreter. Send Jarry to Washington."

"Sarah, you know Jarry is working with the agent. You can write on paper and talk to the Big Father in Washington."

"All right," she said. "I will come to Malheur as soon as I can cross the mountains in my wagon."

As Sarah was preparing for her journey south, two men from Canyon City came to see her. They had heard she was going to the agency and wanted a ride. One of the men had a twelve-year-old daughter. After agreeing upon a fee, Sarah and her passengers set out the following afternoon. Talking with Rosey Morton, who was fascinated by Sarah, made the two-day trip pass pleasantly. Sarah dropped the passengers off at the agent's house, praying Reinhart would not see her, and whipped her team the two miles to her people's camp. She stopped at her cousin Jarry's place.

Exhausted, Sarah slept. When she awoke, chiefs Egan and Oytes were waiting to escort her to the council-tent. There she was introduced to Bannock Jack. The Bannock chief regarded Sarah with skepticism, until Egan told him Sarah was their former interpreter and teacher. And that she had the special gift of education.

"Tell me what the newspapers are saying about our troubles at Fort Hall," Bannock Jack asked Sarah.

She explained she had been living a long way from Fort Hall and had not seen the newspapers.

"You can talk on paper," the Bannock chief said. "Will you write down all that I will tell you?"

Egan fetched pencil and paper for Sarah and a board to serve as a desk. She took down the Bannock's account of the killing of the two white men. The chief's version echoed what Natchez had told her earlier. Bannock Jack added that the whites took the Bannocks' ponies and guns and said they would kill them all if the Bannock murderers were not turned in within ten days. The Bannock warriors were caught and imprisoned, along with other tribesmen, and sentenced to death.

"The friends of the prisoners are on the warpath," the chief concluded. "They want to kill the soldiers."

Sarah looked up from her lap-desk. Was this the beginning of the great war Natchez mentioned? Would all the tribes rise up with the Bannocks to kill the whites? This was grave news indeed. She wished her father were there to advise them.

"Do we not have just cause?" said the chief. "We did not refuse to get the men who killed the whites. We did as they asked. Now they punish us by taking our ponies and guns and say they will kill us all anyway."

Bannock Jack asked Sarah to send the report to the Big Father in Washington so they could get back their guns and ponies. She promised to do so.

The council was not over. Egan stood up to speak. "My dear mother," he began.

Sarah blinked with surprise. Her people only addressed superiors as dear mothers or dear fathers. She had not expected to be addressed by such a title until she was quite old. Her ability to talk on paper had elevated her status! She enjoyed the buoyant feeling of being recognized as an important woman.

Egan told her about living conditions on the reservation since she had left. Sarah could plainly see her people were suffering. He ended his speech with a plea to the men assembled in the tent to give Sarah all their money, so she could go to Washington and ask the Big Father for help.

Immediately the men emptied their pouches. Coins fell at Sarah's feet. When the money was counted, it came to twenty-nine dollars and twenty-five cents. A very small sum. But looking at the hopeful faces of her people, Sarah could not refuse.

"I will be only too happy to do all I can in your behalf," she said.

Sarah decided to go first to Elko, Nevada, and sell her team and wagon. She could buy a swift horse and ride as far as she could to Washington, saving her money for train fare later. Mr. Morton needed to go to Silver City, Idaho. Sarah agreed to take him and Rosey for a fee of fifty dollars. Now she would have a little more cash for that long journey East.

The next morning they set off. Sarah perched tensely on her wagon seat, alert for danger. For three days, they crossed the barren countryside with no sign of an Indian war. But it was ominously silent. They passed empty houses along the road.

"Why do you suppose no one is living in those houses?" Rosey Morton asked Sarah. "Why have they all gone away?"

"I do not know," Sarah replied, but her heart fluttered with fear. It was too quiet, too still.

On the fourth day, on the summit of the Owyhee

Mountains, a man standing in the road wildly flagged them down.

Sarah stopped the team. "What is it?" she asked.

"Indian war!" he cried. "The Bannocks are on the warpath, killin' everything in their way!"

Sarah raced her team down the slope. At the stage-road, they met three more men who said their stage driver had been murdered. Sarah told them who she was and asked for news.

"There's fighting going on at South Mountain," one of the men reported. "A lot of Indians were killed. Paiutes, too."

"Are the Paiutes also on the warpath?" Sarah asked. She could not believe her father would ever agree to go to war. Even if the Bannocks had just cause, he would not sacrifice the lives of his men in a futile war.

"No, your people are fighting the Bannocks with the whites. But the Bannocks whipped them. They are all at the storehouse." He tipped his head back to look at her from under his hat brim. "I'd advise you not to go any farther. The Bannocks want nothing better than to kill Chief Winnemucca's daughter."

Sarah never doubted the man spoke the truth. She slapped the harness with an urgent crack. They reached the storehouse late that night. Soldiers came out with raised guns. Sarah and the Mortons put their hands up to show they were unarmed. The soldiers stared at her as if she were some fearful beast.

Captain Bernard demanded to know her business.

"I am Sarah Winnemucca, daughter of Chief Winnemucca," she said. "I am going to Elko, Nevada. The man and girl riding with me are on their way to Silver City."

The captain said warily, "We have reason to believe you are carrying ammunition in that wagon."

Now Sarah realized her precarious position. The soldiers thought she was aiding the enemy! "Go and see for yourself, captain. If you find anything besides a knife and a pair of scissors I will give you my head for a football. How can I be taking guns to my people when I am going away from them?"

Then she told him of her mission to Washington. Captain Bernard nodded, convinced of her sincerity, and canceled his order to search her wagon.

From a Numa scout who called himself Paiute Joe, Sarah learned what had happened at South Mountain.

"The Bannocks were killing everything and everybody, whites and Indians. The soldiers came on Buffalo Horn's camp and fought with them. Then they ran away and left the scouts at the mercy of the Bannocks," the Paiute scout said. "I jumped off my horse and fired at Buffalo Horn as he came galloping up. He fell and his men fled when they saw their chief fall to the ground. I jumped on my horse and came to Silver City."

Sarah understood the significance of Buffalo Horn's death. The Bannocks would stop at nothing to avenge their chief. Her people would also suffer, since they were allied with the whites. The People had been forced to choose sides. Rather than die in droves at the hands of the white army, the Numa sided against the Bannocks. Sarah knew her father had made a difficult decision.

She could not turn her back on her people now. She wanted to help end this war as soon as possible, before more blood was spilled.

"Captain," she said to Bernard. "If I can be of any use to the army, I am at your service."

"Do you know the country well?" Bernard wanted to know.

She nodded.

"I will telegraph General Howard at Fort Boise and see what he says about this."

Sarah had met General Howard once before, when he visited Malheur. He was a good man.

Captain Bernard left, leading his command to Fort Boise.

Later that night, Sarah had second thoughts about her offer to help the army. She lay awake until dawn. What did she think she could do, stop the war herself? The light from a solitary star was very weak indeed. But then she remembered she was the daughter of a chief. She *could* help her people. As daylight brightened her room, her resolve surged back.

At breakfast Rosey Morton burst into tears. "Please don't go with the soldiers, Sarah," she sobbed. "I don't want you to be killed."

Sarah patted the girl's arm. She had no idea the child thought so much of her.

"My daughter speaks for me as well," said Mr. Morton. "Rosey loves you dearly, and I, too, am fond of you. Will you marry me, Sarah? We will go away from here, the three of us."

Sarah was speechless. In a few short hours, she had braved danger, offered her services to the army, and received a marriage proposal! In the bright light of day, her resolve surged back. She gently refused Mr. Morton's proposal and told the soldiers she was ready to serve in whatever way the army needed her.

The army had an assignment for her right away. The soldiers outfitted Sarah with a good horse and she rode north to Fort Boise as hard as she could. At the army post on the Owyhee River, she met with Captain Bernard.

"General Howard says you may work for the army. I need you to take a message to my scouts," he told her. "I want my scouts to find the whereabouts of the hostile Bannocks and take this information to Camp Harney."

Sarah located the Indian scouts, George and John, and relayed the captain's order.

"We are not going near the enemy," George said emphatically. "It is too dangerous. Sarah, they have captured your father and are holding him and some others prisoner. We do not know how many. And your brother Natchez is dead. He was killed trying to escape."

When Sarah learned this shocking news, her heart felt dead within her. Not her big brother! How could he be killed? And what would happen to her father?

She reported back to Captain Bernard. "Your scouts will not go near the Bannock camp. But I will. Send me, captain."

"You!" Bernard cried. "You cannot go — can you?"

"If there is a horse to carry me," she said.

And if there wasn't, she would walk. Nothing would prevent her from trying to save her father.

15

The best place to cross the Owyhee River was about fifteen miles downstream from Fort Boise. Sarah skillfully guided her horse through the rushing water.

"The camp is just ahead," George called to Sarah. He and John, the other Numa scout, accompanied Sarah after all. Sarah figured they were shamed into coming because a woman was willing to go where men were afraid.

As her horse staggered up the steep bank, Sarah patted the oilcloth packet inside her jacket, making sure her letter was safe. It had not been easy to convince Captain Bernard to let her go to the Bannock camp. At last he sent a telegram to General Howard, requesting permission to engage Sarah officially as a scout. General Howard wired back, not only giving permission, but also offering a reward of five hundred dollars if her mission was successful.

"Five hundred dollars!" Sarah had repeated in

astonishment. That would be more than enough money to go to Washington. And the money left over could be used to help her people.

"The general would also like you to get your father and his people to come to us. They will be taken care of and well fed," Captain Bernard had added.

Sarah had heard promises before. But her father's life was at stake now. She asked for a letter that would enable her to get help if she needed it.

Captain Bernard wrote: *To all good citizens in the country: — Sarah Winnemucca, with two of her people, goes with a dispatch to her father. If her horses should give out, help her all you can and oblige. Captain Bernard*

With the letter, rations of hard bread, and a saddle horse, Sarah set out for enemy territory with her escorts.

Soon they reached the camp of the civilian scouts, who were all asleep. Sarah knew the army was paying these men as much as twenty-five dollars a day and this was how they did their job.

She burst into their camp. "Is this the way you find the enemy?" she shouted, swinging off her lathered horse. "We could have killed every one of you if we had been the enemy." Then she demanded a fresh horse, showing them her letter.

Her newfound authority brought results. One of the men saddled the best horse in the camp while another fixed them a hasty dinner of cold beans. Soon they were on their way again.

Not far beyond the river crossing, Sarah spotted the Bannocks' trail. Nudging her horse in that direction, she followed the trail downriver. They had traveled about fifteen miles when they came upon signs of a campsite. Slipping off her horse, Sarah knelt to examine clumps of hair clinging to the brush like black spiderwebs. She picked up a broken shell bead. John came up with remnants of buckskins and tatters of calico.

"Buffalo Horn must have been killed around this place," she concluded. "They cut off their hair and tore their clothes here." She felt a pang — her own father could have been slain. She understood the grief of the hostile tribe and knew they would stop at nothing to avenge their leader's death.

The trail now struck off toward Barren Valley, an aptly named land of hot, dry wind and little vegetation. The ragged peaks of Steens Mountain loomed above the desert floor. Sarah saw something long and black half-coiled around a rock. At first glance she thought it was a huge snake. It was a bullwhip.

"This must have belonged to the stagecoach driver." She tucked the whip into her saddle, hoping the man's death had been swift.

Sensing time might be running out for her father, Sarah pushed on through rocky countryside. Several times her horse stumbled. But she did not allow them to slow down. They rode like demons all day, without stopping for food or water, and continued the same dogged pace long after nightfall. At last, Sarah signaled for them to halt.

"Our horses are weary and will surely fall over and kill us." Trying to lighten the grim situation, she joked, "Then the Bannocks would not have the pleasure of killing us."

They ate hard bread with no water. Sarah was so exhausted she could barely chew. She gave her orders for the night. "John, you stand guard first. Then wake George and let him stand guard the rest of the night. We must start again just as soon as we can see to ride."

Using her saddle as a pillow, Sarah lay down, her horse's bridle tied to her arm. She could not sleep. Her horse kept tugging on her arm and disturbing thoughts kept tugging at the edges of her mind. What if her father was not at the Bannock camp? What if he had already been killed?

When she heard John announce, "It is daylight," she jumped up and threw her saddle on her horse.

"We will leave straightaway," she told them. "I am almost dead for water. We can water our horses and ourselves at Mr. Crawley's ranch. It is not far."

As if understanding her words, the thirsty horses trotted down the trail. It was very quiet, even for that hour of the morning. Sarah strained for a glimpse of the ranch house.

"I cannot see it," she said. Then she saw the burnt-out hulk of the house, smoke curling toward the sky. Fresh tracks told her the house had been burned yesterday morning. The Bannocks were just ahead of them.

"Let us not stop here," George said nervously. "They must be close by." Fear showed on his and John's faces.

"It is of no use to be afraid," Sarah said crisply. "We have to see the enemy and we will. If they kill us, we will die and that is that. Now we must have something to eat." She set about making coffee in a tin can she found in the rubble. Her matter-of-fact attitude bolstered their spirits. John wanted to kill one of the chickens flurrying around the farmyard, but Sarah said they would touch no livestock that did not belong to them. The men obeyed. She was the leader on this trip.

She led the way toward Steens Mountain, where the Bannocks had left a trail of objects — a clock at Juniper Lake, a fiddle several miles farther. At midday, John shot a mountain sheep. They ate the fresh kill, then Sarah, anxious not to waste more time, hurriedly mounted up again.

About five miles past Juniper Lake, Sarah spotted a tall figure running along the mountain ridge. There was something familiar about his loping stride. Rising up in her saddle, Sarah waved a handkerchief.

"Who are you?" the man called.

She recognized her brother's voice. "Your sister, Sarah!"

Lee Winnemucca leaped on his pony and skidded down the steep hillside. He took Sarah in his strong arms. "Dear sister, you have come to save us. We are all prisoners of the Bannocks."

"If you are a prisoner, why are you out here?" she asked.

"They let us out to gather wood and hunt," Lee replied, "but they are in the mountains, looking out. Take off your hat and dress and unbraid your hair." Sarah did as he told her. "Put this blanket around you."

John and George hid their guns and wrapped blankets around themselves. In a short time, they all were dressed like Bannocks.

"How can you all be prisoners?" she wanted to know. "How did this happen?"

Lee explained that the Bannocks ordered Chief Winnemucca to fight with them against the whites. Their father refused to send his good men to death. The Bannocks captured him and threatened to kill him if they fought with the whites. The tribe wouldn't leave their chief and became prisoners in the Bannock camp.

"Where is our father?" Sarah asked.

"We are all up over the mountain."

162

"I must go to him. I have a message for him."

Lee was horrified. "No, Sarah! You will be killed! They will kill anyone that comes with messages from the whites."

"But they won't know me," she insisted.

"Yes, they will. Oytes is their chief now."

Oytes the Bannock chief! She knew the man could not be trusted. Still, she had a mission to fulfill. "I must go to our father. He is all we have left, since Natchez is dead — "

"Natchez is not dead!" Lee said. "He made his escape three days ago after saving the lives of three white men."

"Natchez is alive!" Sarah wanted to shout with joy. If Natchez had risked his life, then how could she, the chief's daughter, do less?

"I must try to save our father and our people," she said in a tone that discouraged further protest. "Now let us go."

The mountain was so steep they had to climb on their hands and knees. At the top, Sarah peered down into the enemy camp. She gasped. More than three hundred lodges were spread over Little Valley. Countless Bannock warriors were catching horses or killing beef cattle. For the first time, Sarah felt a quaver of fear.

How could she, one woman, possibly penetrate such a fortress? If she were caught, it would be instant death.

"Where are our people?" she asked Lee. He

pointed to a large group of tents near the woods. Sarah bit her lip, contemplating. It *might* work.

"We will go in on foot and leave our horses here," she said.

They hurtled down the mountain like antelope. Lee scurried into Winnemucca's tent and whistled when it was safe for Sarah to leave the cover of underbrush.

Inside the tent, her father hugged her. "My dear little girl," he cried. "Have you come to save us?"

"Yes," Sarah whispered. "I have come to save you all, but you must be quiet. Get ready to leave tonight." She hurriedly outlined the plan that came to her while on the mountaintop. "I want the women to make believe they are gathering wood for the night, and then they will slip away. When it is dark, the men can go. Lee, fetch as many horses as you can and drive them into the woods. The women will meet us at Juniper Lake."

The women obeyed, slipping out one by one with ropes for the horses. Word of the escape plan passed from tent to tent. When it was completely dark, Sarah crept out of the tent, followed by Lee, the Numa scouts, and her father.

They crawled through the camp. Sarah's legs felt heavy, as if she were in a dream. Her father pulled her along when she stumbled. Miraculously, none of the hostiles noticed them. Sarah almost screamed when she heard a noise. It was Mattie, Lee's wife, with a horse for them. On one horse, she and her father scrambled up the mountain, where Sarah had left her own horse. When everyone was mounted, they rode like the wind to Juniper Lake.

The People were waiting, afraid the Bannocks were following.

"There is not a minute to lose," Sarah urged. "We have many miles before us. Women, tie your children to your backs, for we must travel all night."

Winnemucca added his own orders. "Ride two by two. Six men keep back in the event we are followed."

Sarah and her father led the column. By daybreak they had reached Summit Springs. They had put enough distance between themselves and the Bannock camp to stop for a while. Mattie brought Sarah some meat she had cooked the night before and brought along. Sarah ate like a starved creature.

Just then a warning whistle shrilled the morning stillness. Wiping her hands on her skirt, Sarah jumped on her horse and galloped to meet the scout who sounded the alarm.

"We are followed by Bannocks!" he cried.

Sarah wheeled her horse back to camp. "Saddle up! They are coming!"

When the scout caught up to them, he told Winnemucca that Egan's group had been overtaken by the enemy.

"I saw Lee running and the Bannocks firing at him. I think he is killed," the man reported. "I heard Oytes say, 'Bring Sarah's head. I will show Sarah Winnemucca who I am.'"

Oytes would always want to be on the winning side, Sarah thought. She wished the traitor had been dealt with at Malheur.

The chief moaned, "My son is killed! I will go back and be killed, too. If we are to pay for what the white people have done to the Bannocks, then let us get it over with."

Sarah stamped her foot. "Father, this is no time for fool talk. I am going back to the troops. What shall I tell General Howard? Do you wish to stay here and be killed or do you want the army's protection?"

Her father looked at her in surprise. His little girl did not seem so very little now. "Tell him to send his soldiers to protect me and my people," he said.

As Sarah was about to leave, Mattie rode up. "Please let me go with you, Sarah. If my husband is dead, why should I stay?"

Off they galloped, over the hot, dry hills and valleys. For seventy-five miles they rode with no water. Sarah was amazed at Mattie's strength. They sang and prayed to the Great

Father to see them safely through this difficult journey.

On the third day, they crossed Muddy Creek and watered their exhausted horses. Letting their horses rest, the women gathered a few white currants, all they could find to eat. Then they remounted and jumped across the stream. A few hours later, they reached the crossing of Owyhee River. Soldiers saw them coming and gave them coffee and hard bread while they saddled fresh horses.

Barely catching their breath, Sarah and Mattie raced the last fifteen miles to the army post. Captain Bernard was waiting for them. He helped the women dismount, shaking his head with amazement as Sarah told him the whole story about helping her people escape from the Bannock camp.

Soldiers nearby exchanged looks of disbelief. Captain Bernard said, "Sarah, that's nearly two hundred and fifty miles."

"Yes, it is true!" she cried. "I have been in the saddle night and day, with no food and little water. I did this for my people. I went where you could not get an Indian man or a white man to go. Now, will you go meet my father and his people? They are on their way here."

"How many of your people?" Bernard asked.

"Nearly seven hundred."

Bernard gave a low whistle. "I think you deserve a hot meal and a good rest, Sarah."

Word of Sarah's heroism reached General Howard. He called her into his office.

"I want you as my interpreter and guide," he said. "I will pay you top wages."

She stood before him, letting his statement sink in. She would be General Howard's personal guide, a demanding job. But she was equal to the task. After all, she had saved her father and her people.

She knew she would feel guilty working against the Bannocks, but no good would come of this war. The days seemed to bring endless difficult decisions. Yet her people would benefit from the money she would earn. She could buy land and build a schoolhouse. She never lost sight of her dream to teach her people.

Before she could build a schoolhouse, though, there had to be peace in the land.

The general was waiting for her answer.

"I accept your offer," she said. "I will work for the army."

16

Sarah bounced along in the wagon-bed, sitting across from Mattie. They were on their way to Camp Lyon. Sarah would have set out for the Bannocks while the trail was fresh, but of course the army had its own way of doing things. The wagon train passed several companies of cavalry.

"I see they have Sarah Winnemucca a prisoner," a soldier joked.

Sarah laughed. It seemed as if everyone knew her as the brave Paiute woman who saved her people and who would now ride with the general.

At Camp Lyon, more troops gathered, and then the assembled army moved on. Sarah felt sorry for the soldiers sweltering in their blue wool uniforms. It was unmercifully hot and dry. The countryside was as inhospitable as any they had encountered — blistering alkali sands and scratchy sagebrush.

One evening in camp, General Howard asked

169

Sarah if she would travel to Camp Harney with a dispatch.

"I am always ready," she said. She was tired, but she had a job to do.

A young lieutenant escorted them, even though Sarah had protested that she and Mattie could travel faster alone. Sarah knew many shortcuts through the rugged terrain. They stopped once at a farmhouse. The farmer's wife was reluctant to feed Sarah, even at the lieutenant's insistence. Sarah could not eat a bite under the woman's hateful gaze. Why did some white women despise her so, when she was risking her life to help the army?

All night they rode, arriving late to Camp Harney. This time Sarah was too tired to eat, but she was grateful to Major Downing's wife, who gave her a new dress to wear. Sarah's old dress was in tatters. When they learned that Captain Bernard was engaged with the enemy some forty-five miles away, they rode back to Captain Howard with the news. With no sleep, Sarah returned to Camp Harney with the general. She and Mattie stopped once to unearth a hidden supply of hard bread and canned baked beans.

"Just think of it," Sarah said to Mattie. "These beans were baked in Boston. A man told me it costs one dollar for a plate of these very beans if you eat them in Boston."

Three days later, they overtook the troops. Volunteer scouts dashed in to report Indian sightings.

Sarah told General Howard, "If you find any Indians within ten hundred miles of here you may say Sarah is telling lies."

"Do you think the scouts are not telling the truth?"

"That is what I mean."

Sarah wondered if the general doubted her ability. She had a chance to prove herself later that day. She and Mattie had pulled ahead of the advancing column. High on a hill, they saw something. They knew what it was, but the soldiers would not.

The bugle sounded "Halt." Sarah rode back to where the scout captain was speaking to General Howard.

"Don't you see them on that hill yonder?" the scout asked. "They have a good place to fight us."

The general turned to Sarah. "What have you to say now? The Indians certainly seem to be there."

"They *seem* to be there, but they are not," she said. "Those are but rocks set about to deceive you."

General Howard could not see well enough through his field glasses. He sent some men up the hill, who soon came back, sheep-faced. The "Indians" were indeed rocks.

"That is a trick our people use," Sarah said. "In this way we gain time to get away from our enemy."

The next day they pressed on, painfully dragging the wagons through impassable mountain ranges. Sarah knew the Bannocks had fresh horses and could outride these poky wagons in an eye-blink. One day they traveled in unbearable heat; the next it was cold and snowing. They passed a large enemy campsite where Sarah found a scalp, the first she had ever seen. Her people did not perform such barbarian acts. How many more lives would this senseless war claim?

They were closing in slowly on the enemy. At Pilot Rock, Sarah informed the general they had passed the Bannocks. They were just on the other side of the Blue Mountains.

General Howard asked her, "Will you go to the enemy and ask if they will surrender?"

Without hesitation, she said she would. She would do anything to end this war. But later that night, General Howard vetoed the plan. "If you should get killed, your father would blame me," he said.

The general placed his troops at Birch Creek and positioned the Gatling gun some distance farther. Sarah told him the Bannocks, who were high above them, could escape into the woods, but Howard believed his troops would take care of them.

When the bugle sounded the signal to fire, Sarah felt the blood drain from her limbs. She was witnessing an actual battle! As guns boomed, she could hear the braves singing as they ran lightly up and down the mountainside, seemingly oblivious to the rain of bullets.

Howard's troops chased the Bannocks back into the woods, where Sarah had predicted they would flee. The next morning, the fight continued. Under the hot sun, the men fired volley after volley. Sarah wanted to help the thirsty troops and help the enemy at the same time. Once again, her loyalties were torn. She could not bear to see any Indian hurt, yet she could not condone the senseless killings of white citizens either.

"Get behind the rocks!" the general called to her. "You will get hit!"

Just then Sarah heard a familiar voice call out from the brush. "Come on, you white dogs! What are you waiting for?" It was Oytes, now chief of the Bannocks.

"Let me go to the front," Sarah said. "I can hear what Oytes is saying."

The general agreed and Sarah leaped on her horse. She raced up the hill near the Gatling gun and listened, but Oytes did not speak again.

The battle lasted about four hours. When it was over, the ground was strewn with spent cartridges, but not a single Bannock had been killed. One soldier was fatally wounded. Sarah sat with him that long night until he died.

Hot on the trail of the Bannocks' rear guard, the troops followed them to a canyon north of the

John Day River. The walls, over one thousand feet deep, were so sheer the men slid down into the stream below. On the steep ascent, the pack animals fell over backward into the stream. Sarah could barely pick up the confusing zigzag threads of the ancient trail.

The Bannocks had time to prepare for an ambush. They opened fire and Captain Bernard hurriedly positioned his troops. By the time the formation was complete, the Indians had fled again. Sarah could understand the officer's frustration. The enemy used the difficult terrain to their advantage.

A baby Bannock girl was found lying facedown on the trail. Captain McGregor fed her gingersnaps and sugar water until Sarah was called over.

"I don't know what to do with this baby," the captain said, gratefully handing the bundle to Sarah. "She's yours."

Sarah smiled at him. "I will tell you how to take care of her," she teased.

"Not me!" The captain left.

"So you have a baby now," General Howard said to her. "I will order some condensed milk. Save her little shirt and beads. We might find her mother."

Two Bannock women had also been captured. Sarah asked one if she would take care of the baby for her. The woman agreed and Sarah showed her how to fix the baby's milk. All the soldiers asked

Sarah about her baby. She was touched at their kindness.

A couple of Umatilla warriors rode into camp to confer with General Howard. The Umatilla Indians acted as if they wanted to help the army, but Sarah regarded them with suspicion. She did not trust them, especially since they demanded high fees for their scouting services. She learned that Egan, the Numa chief recaptured by the Bannocks during the great escape, was now fighting with the Bannocks. She could not believe Egan would turn against her father this way.

The troops were out of supplies. Their command joined the other troops scattered about the countryside to wait for the commissary wagons. Then they were off in pursuit of the Bannocks, down the Granite Creek Valley, on to Burnt River Meadows, over Ironsides Mountain, past Canyon City, and over Castle Rock Mountain, never stopping.

Sarah was exhausted. "I am so tired!" she told General Howard. "Can Mattie and I stop a while and rest?"

The general shook his head regretfully. "I am afraid something might happen to you, Sarah."

She did not think she could take another step. "Please. We must rest one night."

General Howard relented and she and Mattie made a hasty camp. Sarah fell asleep almost instantly and dreamed that Egan was brutally murdered, his head cut off, his body chopped into pieces. She screamed until Mattie shook her awake.

"What is the matter?" Mattie asked.

"Egan," Sarah said. "He is dead. I know it."

She and Mattie rejoined Howard's command the next day. They rode near the Malheur Reservation. Sarah did not see any of her people. The marches grew longer. Thirty miles one day, forty the next, just to reach water. Horses dropped in their tracks and the soldiers had to walk. Sarah knew the location of a secret spring about twenty miles away. They rode in the searing heat, without a sign of another human.

That night, Sarah saw the distant flare of a signal-fire. The officers were immediately up in arms.

"It is the signal-fire of distress and loneliness," Sarah told them. "It was built by just one Indian."

Scouts brought the man down from the hills. To Sarah it seemed as if gains were made one man at a time. The war dragged on with the summer. The army's noose closed in on the hostiles and finally the main fighting was over except for a few minor skirmishes. The Bannocks surrendered.

Sarah was so glad, she cried. At last the fighting was over.

Next began the difficult job of rounding up the defeated Bannocks. Sarah rode beside General

Howard with the baby strapped in a cradleboard. At every camp she asked if the child belonged to anyone. At the last camp, she saw a young woman with recently shorn hair. The woman's torn clothing indicated she was in deep mourning.

Sarah approached her with the baby dressed in the yellow shirt and beads. "Does anyone know who this child belongs to?"

The woman cried out with joy. "Oh, my baby, my lost little girl! Thank you for saving my baby."

The officers had named the baby after Sarah, and the Bannock woman kept the name. Sarah was happy to reunite a mother and child, after witnessing so many separated families.

Another story did not have such a happy ending. Sarah learned that her nightmare came true: Egan, the Numa chief who supposedly had turned traitor, had been murdered in just the way she had dreamed by U-ma-pine, chief of the Umatilla Indians.

Wearied by the long campaign, Sarah asked General Howard for a leave. "I want to go to Camp McDermitt to see my father. Mattie will serve as your interpreter."

Sarah galloped the seventy miles to Camp McDermitt. Riding into the compound at daybreak, she roused the sleeping People. "You are sleeping too much! Get up!"

"Who is it? What is it?" a woman said, jumping up.

Sarah pounded on to her brother's tent. "Hello! Get up. The enemy is at hand!"

Natchez stumbled out of his sleeping robe. "Sarah!" he cried. "Wife, make a fire. Bring my sister a blanket."

Another man brought Sarah the blanket.

"Lee!" she cried. "You are alive!"

"As you can see," he said, teasing her. "It is not so easy to kill a Winnemucca."

Sarah's heart sang with happiness. Her family was safe!

The People sleepily stirred to life.

Natchez said, archly, "My people, I hope you have passed the beautiful night in peaceful sleep. I am sorry to say that no one has come to say there is no enemy here. I am afraid, my young men, you are not doing your duty. For I have here in my camp a warrior. Come and see for yourself."

Winnemucca was the first to arrive. When he recognized his daughter, he ran to her and gathered her in his arms. "Oh, my poor child. I thought I never would see you. Look at me. Let me see if it is really my daughter."

Tears streamed down his lined cheeks. Her father had aged since she had last seen him. Sarah could not hold back her own tears.

She told them everything — about the baby, the endless dry marches, sitting with the dying soldier, her dream about Egan and the horrible truth about his death. When she had finished her tale, her father rose and said to the assembly:

"I am ashamed to speak to you, my children. I am ashamed for you, not for myself. Where is one among you who can get up and say, 'I have been in battle and have seen soldiers and my people fight and fall.' Shame to you, young men, who ought to have come with this news to me.

"How thankful I am that a child of mine has saved so many lives. Her name is far beyond yours. Hereafter we will look on her as a chieftain, for who is worthy to be chief but her."

A lump rose in Sarah's throat. Among her people, there had never been a woman chief before. She was the first. But most important, she was honored in the eyes of her father. There would be no more disagreements between them. From this day forward, they would work together to help their people.

That fall, the Big Father in Washington ordered all the People to Camp Harney before being sent to a reservation. The People were upset. They did not want to be at Reinhart's mercy again.

Young Chief Leggins came to Sarah. "You, our mother, must talk to the soldiers and tell them we cannot go to Malheur. Will you go do this for us?"

Sarah wondered when the trouble would end. Always she would do the best she could for her people. She could not do any less — she was their chief.

"Yes," she said, saddling her horse. "I will go."

Perhaps this time she would be able to get her people settled happily and pursue her own dream.

As Sarah cantered down the trail, she saw a vision: a sturdy, red-painted schoolhouse on a tree-shaded knoll. Inside, she could see the excited faces of Numa children as they opened their first books and beheld the secrets of the world.

Epilogue

Life for the Paiutes did not improve after the Bannock uprising. Wrongly including the innocent Numa with the hostile Bannocks, officials in Washington ordered all tribes involved to be sent far away, where they could not cause any more trouble.

Sarah was asked to accompany her people to Yakima, Washington, in the depths of winter. Women, children, and the elderly were forced to march 350 miles through deep snows, over mountains, and across icy rivers. Many froze to death. At the prisoner camp, the People were herded into cattle sheds with no food. That summer, the survivors labored in the wheat fields.

The People begged Sarah to go East and talk to the Big Father in Washington. Sarah set out for San Francisco to earn money for the trip. Dressed as an Indian princess, she packed lecture halls with her eloquent talks about the trials of her people.

On January 19, 1880, Sarah, her father, and her brother Natchez arrived in Washington, DC. She met with Interior Secretary Carl Shurz, who claimed he would send canvas for tents, free the Yakima prisoners, and give land to each Paiute family. Sarah briefly saw President Hayes, the "Big Father," on this trip.

The tent canvas never arrived and Schurz's promise to free the People in Yakima proved to be worthless. Feeling betrayed by the government, Sarah could not blame her people from turning away from her.

She worked at Fort Vancouver as a teacher and interpreter a few years, then went to visit her sister Elma in Montana. There Sarah married a white man, Lambert Hopkins. Her father died while she was living in Montana. The People at Pyramid Lake asked for her help again.

This time Sarah took their cause to New England, lecturing in Boston to a sympathetic audience. She wrote a book, *Life Among the Paiutes: Their Wrongs and Claims*, published in 1883, the first book by a Native American written in English.

With her earnings and contributions, Sarah opened a school for Indians near Lovelock, Nevada, the realization of a lifelong dream. She taught the children practical skills like cooking and digging a cellar in addition to their studies in reading, writing, and "figuring." Her school was a success, praised by journalists and educators. Sarah added to the contributions by lecturing, but eventually ran out of funds and was forced to close the school.

Sarah's husband died of tuberculosis. A few years later, she went back to Montana to visit Elma. On October 17, 1891, the light of a solitary star was suddenly extinguished. Sarah Winnemucca Hopkins died, at age 47, possibly of tuberculosis.

"I mean to fight for my downtrodden race while life lasts," she wrote in her book. For more than thirty years, her dedication to her people had never wavered.

About the Author

CANDICE F. RANSOM lives in Centreville, Virginia, with her husband, where she writes books for young people.

Her popular Kobie books are based on her own experiences growing up. Ms. Ransom says, "My brain stops at about age fifteen. I'm a grown-up by default." Some of her books include, *Going on Twelve; Thirteen; Fourteen and Holding; Fifteen at Last; My Sister, the Meanie; My Sister, the Traitor; My Sister, the Creep; Millicent the Magnificent;* and *So Young To Die.*